Eduard Moerike

MOZART ON THE WAY TO PRAGUE

Eduard Moerike

Mozart
on the way to
Prague

TRANSLATED BY WALTER AND CATHERINE

ALISON PHILLIPS

DRAWINGS BY SUZANNE EINZIG

WESTHOUSE
LONDON
1946

on the way to

TRANSLATED BY WALTER AND CATHERINE

WESTHOUSE
1946

First published in July 1946 by
JOHN WESTHOUSE (PUBLISHERS) LIMITED
49 Chancery Lane London

Printed by
KENNERLEY PRESS LIMITED
1-4 Britannia Walk
London N 1

INTRODUCTION

TO ENGLISH READERS the name of Eduard Mörike is perhaps best known as that of the Württemberg ex-pastor whose verses inspired so many lovely songs by Schumann, Brahms, Robert Franz and, chief of all, Hugo Wolf. His exquisite poems, his self-revealing study of the young artist 'Maler Nolten,' and his delightful letters are well known to lovers of German literature; while in his own country this short story, 'Mozart auf der Reise nach Prag,' has become a classic – as English examination students know to their cost, for Mörike's characteristic idiom, a thing of subtle nuances and tantalizingly artful simplicities, almost defies the translator.

From his early youth the Swabian poet was an enthusiast for music in general and Mozart in particular, and delighted, to use the expressive German phrase, in 'living himself into' the composer's life and age, projecting himself imaginatively into his personality, and studying his creative processes in the light of his own. Though this story did not appear till 1855 the idea of it was in his head as early as 1847, when he wrote to a friend: 'I simply cannot believe it possible to write a really enjoyable (*genussreich*) biography of Mozart. Indeed, a fragment of imaginative composition (*Dichtung*) taken from his life, such as you once had in mind, would be a thousand times more satisfying.' The subject continued to occupy his attention at intervals, and in the summer of 1852 he wrote his wife the following account of a drive to Wimsheim, where he was going to take a cure: 'We drove along the beautiful roads . . . finding the cool air most beneficial, and each of us quietly absorbed in pleasant meditations. . . . In sight of Rutesheim, as I was pursuing the idea of my Novelle, I had a strong inrush of imaginings about Mozart . . .; you will recognize them one day from the "trombones of silver," and you must associate them with that passage in your mind.'

We see, then, that what is perhaps the finest passage in the story, and forms in some sort its culminating point, the description of the finale in 'Don Giovanni,' was in his mind from the first. It remained to build up round this noble tribute to Mozart's genius that 'picture of the artist's individuality' which it was his object to present – as we learn from the letter sent with a presentation copy of King Maximilian II of Bavaria on the occasion of Mozart's jubilee – while at the same time suggesting to the reader 'a feeling of touched melancholy, despite the prevailing brightness of the atmosphere, or rather, by reason of that very quality.'

After many interruptions the story gradually took shape, and Mörike was able to read it to the poet Theodor Storm and other good judges. Large portions of the original draft were omitted when, in July and August, 1855, it was published in instalments in Cotta's 'Morgenblatt,' afterwards appearing in the form of a brochure towards the end of the same year. It met with such a warm reception that Theodor Storm, who introduced it to many of his friends, was able to send Mörike a letter of almost hysterical eulogy from a worthy Landrat, who declared that he was in a perfect 'Paroxismus' of admiration. Since then numerous éditions de luxe bear witness to its continued popularity in its own country.

Since the story contains a number of allusions to certain events in Mozart's career, it may be well first to recall these briefly. At the time when the story opens, in the autumn of the year 1787, Mozart's opera 'The Marriage of Figaro' had been cheated of its success in Vienna by the cabals of his enemies, most important among whom was Salieri, chief Kapellmeister at the Opera, who had the ear of the Emperor Joseph II and encouraged his taste for the lighter type of Italian opera. In spite of this it had created a furore at the Prague Opera-house, for which Mozart had accordingly been invited to compose another work. The result of this invitation was 'Don Giovanni,' the libretto for which, as for 'Figaro,' was composed by Lorenzo da Ponte. Once more Mozart's music triumphed in Prague, but at first met with small success in Vienna, where the Emperor is said to have remarked that it was 'too much for the teeth of his good Viennese.' Indeed, his works found serious rivals in such now forgotten operas as

'Una Cosa rara,' by the Catalan Vicente Martin y Solar, or Salieri's 'Tartar,' the libretto of which, like that of 'Figaro,' was based on a work of Beaumarchais. Not till late in 1787 did his work as a composer of more than chamber-music receive official recognition from the Emperor, when, instead of succeeding to the position of second Kapellmeister left vacant by the death of Gluck, he was appointed Kammerkompositor to the Emperor at a salary which, as he bitterly remarked, was 'too much for what I do produce, but too little for what I could produce.'

Mozart is here shown driving with his wife to Prague for the production of his still unfinished opera. They stop at a village, Mozart wanders into the grounds of a local magnate, and in a fit of absentmindedness, plucks an orange from a cherished tree with a romantic history. This incident, which nearly has an unfortunate ending, brings about his introduction to the Count's family instead, and, by a train of association, suggests to him a melody for his opera. In the gay setting of this eighteenth-century plea-sure-house, among the cultured, genial, music-loving nobility who were his best patrons, a more serious note is struck as Mozart plays them the grim finale of his 'Don Giovanni'; and through all the music, gaiety and laughter, the episodes and anecdotes both comic and romantic, there runs like a sombre accompaniment the haunting premonition of the composer's death, till the story closes on a note of doom and sadness.

It has been criticized as containing too much that is purely biographical, which, it is claimed, does not blend sufficiently well with the fantastic and imaginative elements. But in order to give a complete presentment of his hero, Mörike seems to have aimed at illuminating him, as it were, from both within and without. Though he did not read the biography of Mozart by Nissen (the second husband of Frau Konstanze Mozart) till his own story was finished – partly, as he confesses, out of indolence, but partly from an 'instinctive anxiety' not to disturb his own 'inward conception' of the man – he had evidently steeped himself in the period and collected all the information he could about the composer's character and idiosyn-crasies. The picture he draws of his personality, at least, tallies in almost every detail with that given, for instance, in Otto Jahn's great biography, or, to cite a more generally accessible authority, the article in Grove's 'Dictionary.'

But, whether justifiably or not, Mörike cherished a sense of affinity with the composer, and in attempting to elucidate the processes of Mozart's genius by the aid of his own views on the relation between the pictorial sense and poetic or musical creation, he was interpreting in the light of his own artistic experience a genius for whom he felt a particular sympathy. In 'Maler Nolten,' which his friends recognized as possessing a strongly autobiographical element, he gives a striking instance of a similar psychological phenomenon to that described in the story. The young painter, a while under the influence of a severe emotional crisis, rides out into the country, and though his mind is still too thoroughly numbed by the shock to think consecutively, he finds himself 'constantly pursued by an absurd, monotonous melody, with which some kobold teasingly harassed his ears in most untimely fashion. . . . And while he was in this dreamy, dizzied state, in place of this uncanny musical visitation (*musikalische Spukerei*) . . . his excited power of imagination brought him with inconceivable rapidity a whole host of pictorial (*malerisch*) situations, which he was impelled to represent to himself in a disjointedly dramatic form, actively accompanied by poetical words, and sketch them roughly in broad outline.'

The mysterious problem of the relation between the various arts, was, of course, a favourite theme of the Romantics, as also of Baudelaire, Rimbaud and the French Symbolists in later days; but though Mozart's description of the fantastic masque on the Bay of Naples, which Mörike represents as having suggested the duet between Masetto and Zerlina in 'Don Giovanni,' is described by one of the noble company as a 'painted symphony,' there is not the slightest suggestion of any theory of 'correspondences' (*Uebereinkunft*) such as was enunciated, for example, by Hoffmann, and afterwards elaborated by Baudelaire, according to which a definite psychical affinity exists between certain sounds, colours and perfumes respectively, so that, as Hoffmann says: 'colours, perfumes and rays of light appear (to the musician) as musical sounds (*Töne*) . . . Just as, in the words of a clever physicist, hearing is an inward seeing, so to the musician seeing becomes an inward hearing, that is, a most intimate consciousness of that music which, vibrating in consonance with his spirit, emanates in sound (*ertönt*) from all that is grasped by his eye.'

In connexion with this Neapolitan masque, at least, Mörike has no mystical or pseudo-scientific theories to propound. His idea seems to be that the character of the creative stimulus is determined by a simple association of ideas, certain visual impressions, accompanied by musical ones of a certain type, being sorted up for years, only to pour forth in melody and harmony when the sight of the orange, plucked in the garden of the 'Italian villa,' stirs the artist's memory and releases a flood of music similar in character to that which he had then heard. But when we come to the fine passage on the finale, the deeper mysteries of music are approached more nearly, and the shadow of death, which has hovered over the story even in its sunny beginnings, grows deeper as Mozart 'leads us into the depths of the spirit realm' and 'fear closes round us.' It is hardly possible to discuss the phenomena of musical creation, especially in connexion with Mozart, without referring to the famous letter which has been quoted in so many psychological and other works as an authentic and highly illuminating document coming from his hand.* Otto Jahn has devoted one of his learned appendices to proving most convincingly that this letter, originally published by Rochlitz in the 'Allgemeine musickalische Zeitung,' cannot be accepted as genuine; but he does not exclude the possibility that it may have been fabricated by Rochlitz on the strength of authentic conversations reported to him by friends of Mozart. The portion of the letter bearing on our subject is as follows:

'When I am all by myself and in a good humour – for instance, when travelling in a carriage, or taking a walk after a good meal, and at night when I cannot sleep, then ideas come to me best and come in streams. Whence and how I do not know, nor can I do anything about it. . . . But those which have occurred to me I store up in my head, and hum them over to myself, too – so others have told me, at least. And now that I have

---

* Mr C. R. Oldman kindly informs me that he has found this passage quoted in the works of Rufus Jones, Sorley, Clutton Brock, Dean Inge, Royce and others.

got firm hold of it, soon one thing after another occurs to me for which such a crumb might be used, in order to make a whole pie (*Pastete*), in accordance with counterpoint, the timbre of the various instruments, etc.

'And this inflames my soul – that is, supposing I am not disturbed; then it grows and grows, and I go on expanding it, making it ever clearer and broader, and the thing really becomes almost complete in my head, even when it is long, so that afterwards I can view it in my mind at a single glance, like a fine picture or a beautiful person, and hear it in my imagination, not as it has come, but, as it were, the whole thing together at the same time. And what a revel that is (*Das ist nun ein Schmaus*)! All the invention and making of it goes on within me as in a fine, strong dream: but best of all is the hearing of the whole thing altogether. And what has thus come into being I do not easily forget again, and that is perhaps the best gift that our Lord God has ever bestowed upon me. So when I come to write it down afterwards, I take from out of my brain, as though out of a bag, that which, as I have said, has previously collected in it. And that, too, is why it comes out afterwards on to the paper fairly rapidly, for, as I have said, it is really complete already, and rarely turns out very different from what it was in my head before. And this, too, is why I suffer myself to be disturbed while writing, however many things may be going on around me: I write all the same, and am even able to chatter the while, for instance about fowls and geese, or about Gretel and Bärbel and so forth. But how it comes that in process of my work my things take on such a form or mannerism that they are Mozartian and not in the manner of anybody else: why, this must be for the same reason as makes my nose just so big and prominent as to be Mozartian and not like other people's noses!'

If Mörike had seen this letter, as is quite possible, he could hardly have failed to notice the resemblance between the symptoms which it describes as accompanying the creative process and those experienced by himself, as related in the above extract from 'Maler Nolten.' It may be added that they are also akin to the mental state and physical symptoms described in Professor Housman's Leslie Stephen Lecture delivered at Cambridge on May 9, 1933. The Mozart-Rochlitz letter, the 'Maler Nolten' extract, Pro-

fessor Housman's amusing analysis, all agree that the moments most propitious for artistic creation seem to be those in which the reasoning faculty
is in abeyance and the unconscious can assert its sway – whether the rest-
less brain be numbed by shock or lulled to repose by exercise and physical
well-being. 'It is at moments like this that one creates,' said Wagner on
Palm Sunday, 1867, standing by the fountain in the Grütli woods after an
expedition by boat across the Lake of Lucerne; and we are reminded of the
memorable day at Spezia in the autumn of 1853, when, as he lay, sick and
physically exhausted, in a 'trance-like state,' the rush of the waters in
which he dreamt himself to be sinking 'soon presented itself to me in the
musical sounds of the chord of E flat major,' which then proceeded to
break itself up into figures till, on waking from his half-sleeping state, he
realized that what had come to him was the orchestral prelude to 'Das
Rheingold' which he had been trying in vain to find.

Whether the poetic or musical 'secretions' – to use Professor Housman's
word – that are ultimately transmuted into works of art are due to some
previous process of 'conception,' as Hoffmann calls it, which has taken
place in moments of 'ecstasy' or 'consecration', what is the precise im-
pulse that causes the unconscious mind to 'proceed from incubation
(Brüten) to creation'; whether the artist is thrown into a hypnotic condition induced by shock or the monotonous reiteration of some sight or
sound, or is himself the hypnotist who imposes his will upon Nature, as
upon a medium, forcing her to reveal her secrets in the mystic language of
the arts: all these are interesting and possibly insoluble problems which,
though not directly propounded, are at any rate suggested by the subject
of Mörike's story. But so far neither the Romantic writers nor the more
scientific modern psychologists have really done much more to explain the
processes of artistic creation than supply more or less pregnant analogies
and metaphors. Whether we quote the mystical jargon of Tieck, Wacken-
roder and Hoffmann, or speak of saturation and precipitation, of impregna-
tion and conception, of hypnotism and trance, or of waves and vibrations,
the obscure workings of the creative mind remain an august mystery.

Jahn, while paying a tribute to Mörike's 'grace and delicacy,' and regretting, characteristically, that he 'laid so much stress on the lighter, more worldly side of Mozart's character,' considers it 'scarcely conceivable that a *poet* could have ascribed to Mozart a manner of composition which was as far as it was possible to be from his nature.' While the composer, Robert Franz, on the other hand, on setting to music the poem 'Denk' es, O Seele,' with which this story concludes, wrote that Mörike had completely dispelled the 'Philistine atmosphere' with which Jahn's monumental work had 'obscured the figure of the composer,' and produced a 'remarkably clarifying effect' upon his own ideas, rendering 'mirror-bright and clear again' what had been dim before. In presence of such differences of opinion, it is perhaps more profitable simply to observe with what art Mörike himself renders into poetical prose the musical quality and emotional effect of Masetto and Zerlina's gay duet on the one hand, and the finale, with its ominous terrors, on the other – two famous passages which may compare with the most penetrating expressions of musical effects in prose by Hoffmann, Tieck or Schumann. Though we may conclude that, after all, Mörike has thrown more light upon the workings of his own creative processes than on those of Mozart, his work is certainly an attractive illustration of that 'generative power' (*zeugende Kraft*) which Goethe held to be inherent in a supreme degree in the works of Mozart – a force which 'goes on working from generation to generation, and is hardly likely to be exhausted and dissipated for a long time to come.'

C. P.

MOZART ON THE WAY TO PRAGUE

IN THE FALL of the year 1787 Mozart set out on a journey to Prague in company with his wife, there to produce 'Don Giovanni.'

By the third day on the road, the fourteenth of September, towards eleven in the morning, the pair were still scarce more than thirty leagues from Vienna, driving in high spirits towards the north-west, having left behind the Mannhardsberg and the German Thaya, near Schrems, where the road has all but emerged from the lovely Moravian mountains.

'The conveyance, with its team of three post-horses,' writes the Baroness von T. to her friend, 'an imposing orange-coloured coach, was the property of a certain old Frau von Volkstett, the wife of a general, who seems for long past to have rather plumed herself upon her relations with the Mozart family and the attentions that she had shown it.' This vague description of the vehicle in question can be supplemented with a few more details by one familiar with the taste of the seventeen-eighties. The orange-coloured carriage was painted on either door with posies of flowers in their natural colouring, the panels being framed with a narrow gold fillet, but the paint had still nothing approaching the gloss of the mirror-surfaced varnish used in the workshops of present-day Vienna, nor had the body such full, swelling lines, though it tapered elegantly downwards in a bold curve; add to this a high roof with stiff leather curtains, which for the time being were drawn back.

A few observations may further be added about the costume of the two travellers. The clothes worn by her husband had been chosen frugally by Frau Konstanze with a view to saving the new full-dress garments packed away in the trunk; with his embroidered waistcoat of a rather faded blue he wore his usual brown frock-coat, having a row of large buttons so fashioned that a layer of red-gold tinsel gleamed through a star-patterned network, and with it black silk breeches, stockings, and gilt buckles on his shoes. For the last hour he had gone without his coat on account of the heat, which was abnormal for that month of the year, and sat bare-headed and in his shirt-sleeves, chatting contentedly. Madame Mozart wore a comfortable travelling-dress with pale green and white stripes. The mass of her beautiful light brown hair fell down, half loosed, upon her neck and shoulders. Never in her life had it been marred by powder, but her husband's thick growth, tied back in a queue, was sprinkled for the nonce even more negligently than usual.

They had ascended at a leisurely pace a gently rising slope between the fertile fields which here and there broke the wide expanse of forest, and had now reached the fringe of the wood.

'Through how many forests,' remarked Mozart, 'have we not already passed to-day, yesterday and the day before! I thought nothing of it at the time, least of all did it occur to me to set foot inside them. Let us just get down here, shan't we, dear heart, and pick some of those blue bell-flowers growing so prettily in the shade over there. Postillion, you can breathe your beasts awhile.'

As the two rose to their feet a slight mishap was revealed, which cost the Master a scolding. Thanks to his heedlessness a bottle of costly perfume had come unstoppered, and emptied its contents unobserved over their clothes and the cushioned seats. 'I might have known it,' she wailed; 'the scent had been so strong for a long time past. Alas! a whole bottle of genuine *Rosée d'Aurore*, clean empty! And I was husbanding it like gold.' 'Why, simpleton!' was his consoling reply, 'Don't you see ? In this way, if in no other, your cordial meet for noses divine has done us a good turn. At first we were sitting in a perfect oven, and all your fanning was of no avail; but soon the whole carriage seemed somehow to have grown quite cool. You put it down to the few drops I had sprinkled on my shirt-frill. We felt new life in us and our talk flowed blithely on, instead of our having to droop our heads like sheep in the butcher's cart. And the good of it will remain with us all the way. But now let us hurry and poke our two Viennese noses into these verdant wilds!'

They stepped arm in arm over the roadside ditch, and so at once deep into the gloom of the fir-wood, which soon deepened into a darkness pierced only here and there by a shaft of sunshine striking vividly down on the carpet of velvet moss. The refreshing coolness, in abrupt contrast with the blazing heat outside, might have been dangerous to the heedless fellow but for his companion's forethought. With some difficulty she pressed upon him the garment she had held in readiness. 'Good God! How glorious!' he cried, gazing up at the lofty boles; 'One might be in a church! I feel as though I had never been in a forest, and now I see for the first time what

manner of thing it really is – this whole population of trees ranged side by side! No human hand planted them, they grew up all of their own accord, and here they stay for the simple reason that it is fun to be alive and carry on the business of life together. You see, in my young days I travelled up and down half Europe, I saw the Alps and the ocean, all that is grandest and most beautiful in creation: and now, idiot that I am, I stand by chance in an ordinary fir-wood on the borders of Bohemia, lost in wonder and rapture that such a thing should really exist, and is not, as it were, just *una finzione de' poeti*, a figment of the poets, like your nymphs and fauns and what not, or even a stage forest, either – no! but rooted in the earth and reared to full stature by moisture and the warmth of the sun. This is the home of the deer, with his wondrous branching antlers on his brow, of the tricksy squirrel, the black-cock and the jay.' He stooped and pulled a fungus, praising the splendid, brilliant red of its cap and the delicate whity gills on its underside, and he pocketed an assortment of fir-cones besides.

'One would think,' said his wife, 'that you had never before taken a look twenty paces into the Prater, though it must have like rarities to offer too.'

'The Prater, do you say? *Saprelotte!* How can you so much as name it here? What with coaches, court swords, French dresses and fans, music and all the din in the world, who could ever see anything else there? Why, the very trees, however they may give themselves airs—I don't know how it is, but the beech-mast and acorns strewn about the ground look for all the world like own brothers and sisters to the hosts of derelict corks mixed up with them. From as far as a couple of leagues away the woods reek of waiters and sauces.'

'Did you ever!' she cried. 'And this is the man who knows no greater pleasure than to sup off roast chicken in the Prater!'

When both were once more seated in the carriage, and the road, after running along for a while on the level, now sloped gently downwards where a smiling landscape stretched away till it melted into the more distant mountains, our Master, having sat silent for a while, began once again: 'Truly the earth is fair, and no man need be blamed for wishing to remain on it as long as possible. Thanks be to God, I feel as fresh and well as ever, and shall soon be ready for a thousand things, which will follow one another in due order as soon as my latest work is completed and produced. How many strange and beautiful things there are in the great world beyond, and how many here at home, of which I know simply nothing yet, in the shape of natural wonders, sciences, arts and useful crafts! Your grimy young charcoal-burner over there at his kiln is as clever a fellow as I am about some things, though I must say I feel an inclination and a longing to have a look into this, that and the other, even though it does not happen to be connected, with my own particular stock-in-trade.'

'The other day,' was her reply, I came across your old pocket calendar for the year 'eighty-five; at the end of it you had jotted down three or four notes. First comes this one: ''In the middle of October they cast the great lions in the Imperial foundry;'' and in the second place, doubly underlined: ''Call upon Professor Gattner.'' Who is he?'

'Oh yes, I know; at the observatory – the nice old gentleman who invites me there from time to time. I had long wanted to look at the moon and the little old man in it with you. They have got a mightly great telescope up there now: they say that on the vast disk one can see, so clearly and distinctly that one could almost touch them, mountains, valleys and abysses, and, on the side where the sun does not fall, the shadow cast by the mountains. For two years now I have been intending to pay him a visit, and I have never managed it yet, more's the pity – and more shame to me, too!'

'Well,' she said, 'the moon won't run away. We're going to catch up with lots of things we have missed.'

After a pause, he went on again: 'And isn't it the same with everything? Fie upon me! I dare not think of all one has omitted to do in time, or put off, or left undone – let alone one's duty to God and one's neighbour – I mean in the way of pure enjoyment, the little innocent pleasures that come everyone's way daily.'

Madame Mozart either could not or would not do anything to turn his volatile emotions in a different direction from that in which they were tending more and more, and unfortunately she could only agree with all her heart as he continued with rising agitation: 'Have I ever been able to enjoy a whole hour's happiness even with my children? For me it was always by snatches and *en passant!* I might give the little chaps a ride on my knee, or romp about the room with them for a minute or two, and then *basta!* that was the end of it! I can't recall ever having spent a jolly day in the country together at Easter or Whitsuntide in a garden or a bit of a wood, all to ourselves on the grass, having fun with the children and playing with flowers, so as to become a child again oneself. And all the while life goes rushing and roaring past – Good God! when one really thinks of it, one could almost break out into a cold sweat of terror!'

The self-reproaches to which he had just given utterance led unexpectedly to a most serious talk between the two, in all confidence and affection. We shall not report it in detail, but rather make a general survey of the circumstances which now formed the express and immediate subject of their discussion, now merely loomed in the background of their consciousness.

And here the painful reflexion forces itself upon us that, in spite of all he
experienced, enjoyed and created during his brief span of life, this fiery
being, incredibly sensitive to all the charms of the world and the sublimest
heights to which the boding soul can soar, none the less never in all his life
arrived at an understanding with himself on any stable and entirely satisfactory footing.

Those who are not bent upon probing deeper for the causes of this
phenomenon than these probably lie in reality, will find them, first and
foremost, in those inveterate and apparently insuperable weaknesses which,
not altogether without reason, we are so much inclined to associate, as an
inevitable accompaniment, with all those qualities in Mozart that arouse
our admiration.

The requirements of the man's nature were highly manifold, and his predilection for the pleasures of society, in particular, abnormally strong.
Esteemed and sought after by the most distinguished houses in the city on
account of his incomparable gifts, he seldom or never refused invitations
to festivities, social gatherings or parties. Besides this, he also gratified his
hospitable instincts to the full within his own more immediate circle. A
musical evening such as had long been an institution at his house on a
Sunday, or an informal midday dinner at his bounteous table with a few
friends and acquaintances two or three times a week, were things which
he would not willingly have gone without. Now and then, to the consternation of his wife, he would bring guests home without notice whom he had
met in the street, persons of very unequal worth, amateurs, fellow-artists,
singers and poets. The idle flatterer, whose only merit lay in his constant
flow of high spirits, his wit and his jokes, sometimes of rather a coarse
variety, was as welcome as the intelligent connoisseur and the competent
player. Again, Mozart was in the habit of seeking most of his recreation
outside his own house. Any and every day he was to be found after meals
at the billiard-table in the coffee-house, and often, too, in the evening at
the inn. He was very fond of driving and riding about the country in the

company of friends and, being a consummate dancer, he frequented dances, routs and masked balls, while once or twice a year he thoroughly enjoyed himself at popular festivities, and especially at the open-air ball during St Bridget's Fair, where he masqueraded as Pierrot.

These recreations, now exuberant and boisterous, now attuned to a more quiet mood, were calculated to provide the necessary rest for his mind after periods of tense concentration and a prodigious discharge of force; nor did they fail to convey to him incidentally, by those mysterious channels through which genius unconsciously operates, those subtle and fleeting impressions which fertilize it by the way. Yet since, unhappily, in such hours as these his great object always was to drain the glad moment to the dregs, no other considerations, whether of prudence or of duty, of self-preservation or love of home, were of any weight. Whether enjoying or creating, Mozart was equally regardless of moderation or steady purpose. Part of the night he always devoted to composition. In the early morning he rested from his labours, often lying long abed. Then from ten o'clock onwards, whether on foot or fetched by a carriage, he went the round of his lessons, which occupied, as a rule, some hours of the afternoon as well. 'We toil away for dear life,' as he himself writes to one of his patrons, 'and often enough it is hard not to lose patience. Being a well-accredited cembalist and music-master, one saddles oneself with a dozen pupils, and now and again with an extra one, regardless of whether there is anything more in him, so long as he pays his thaler *per marca* [that is, per lesson]. Any mustachioed Hungarian in the Engineers is welcome who may be visited by Satan with a desire to study thorough-bass and counterpoint for no earthly reason; or else the most impertinent of little countesses, who receives me scarlet with annoyance if by chance I fail to knock at her door on the stroke of the clock, just as if I were Maître Coquerel who curls her hair.' And when, worn out with these and other professional labours, concerts, rehearsals and the like, he pined for fresh air, all that was usually granted to his jaded nerves was the apparent relaxation of a fresh excitement. His constitution was stealthily undermined, and a constantly recurring mood of melancholy was, if not produced, at any rate undoubtedly fostered by the selfsame cause; and thus that premonition of an early death which came at last to dog his every step, met with its inevitable fulfilment. For his part he was inured to worries of every sort and shade, not excepting a sense of remorse, and they brought a tang of bitterness into every pleasure. Yet we know that even these sorrows, too, sublimated and purified, were merged in the deep spring which, welling from a thousand conduits, poured forth inexhaustibly in his changing melodies all the anguish and the bliss of the human heart.

The evil effects of Mozart's way of living showed themselves most plainly in the state of his domestic affairs. The charge of mad and reckless extravagance can easily be understood, for it was the inevitable complement of one of his finest qualities. Anyone who came to him in urgent need, hoping to borrow a sum of money or persuade him to act as surety, generally reckoned in advance upon his omitting to make very thorough enquiries into their pledges or security; in fact, he would not have troubled about such things any more than a child. What he preferred was to give the money then and there, and always with a laughing open-handedness, especially when he believed himself at the moment to have enough and to spare.

Yet the resources required to meet such expenditure in addition to his ordinary household needs were out of all proportion to his income. His earnings from theatres and concerts, publishers and pupils, together with his pension from the Emperor, were still less adequate because public taste was as yet far from having declared definitely in favour of Mozart's music. Such pure loveliness, richness and depth was commonly found repellent by comparison with the easily assimilated fare that had hitherto been so popular. It is true that, while it was being performed, the inhabitants of Vienna could hardly have enough of 'Belmonte und Konstanze' [or 'Die Entführung aus dem Serail'], owing to the popular elements in that piece; yet it was certainly not due solely to the intrigues of the manager that a few years later 'Figaro' unexpectedly proved a sorry fiasco in rivalry with the charming, but greatly inferior 'Cosa rara' – that same 'Figaro' which the more cultivated, or less prejudiced inhabitants of Prague received immediately afterwards with such enthusiasm that, touched and gratified, the Master determined to write his next grand opera specially for them. Despite the unfavourable conditions of the day and the influence of his enemies, with a little more prudence and shrewdness Mozart might still have derived very considerable profits from his art: as it was, his own personal gains were wretched even from those ventures in which the great public perforce applauded him to the echo. In short, all things worked together – fate, character and his own fault – to prevent this unique genius from prospering.

But we can easily understand in what a sad plight any housewife knowing her business must have found herself in such conditions. Though herself young and full of spirits, and, as a musician's daughter, a true-born artist, accustomed, moreover, to privations from childhood upwards, Konstanze showed the greatest good-will in checking the evil at its source, pruning away much that was amiss, and making up for losses on a large scale by economy in small matters. Yet in this last respect she lacked, perhaps, true aptitude and early experience. She had charge of the cash-box and kept the housekeeping-book: all demands, all duns, and any tiresome things that might occur, went to her alone. At times, indeed, her troubles threatened to overwhelm her, especially when, in addition to all this tribulation – to want, painful embarrassments and the dread of public dishonour – were added the low spirits in which her husband was often plunged for a whole day on end, inert and deaf to all consolation, as with sighs and laments, whether at his wife's side or silent and absorbed all by himself in a corner, he pursued like an endless screw a single gloomy idea, the recurring thought of death. Yet she seldom lost heart, and as a rule her clear vision supplied aid and counsel, if only for a time. But essentially there was little or no improvement. Even if by jest or earnest, by prayers or cajolery, she succeeded once in a way in persuading him to have tea with her and enjoy his supper at home with the family without going out afterwards, what did it profit her? Now and then, suddenly conscience-stricken and moved by his wife's tear-stained eyes, he might in all sincerity curse his bad habit and make the finest promises, even more than she asked of him – it was all in vain; he found himself, without intending it, back again in the old ways. One is almost tempted to believe that he could not behave otherwise, and that, had some totally different line of conduct, in keeping with our ideas of what is seemly and fitting for all men, been somehow imposed upon him by force, it must surely have ruined the most essential qualities of that wondrous nature.

Yet Konstanze continued to hope for a favourable turn in the state of affairs, in so far as this could come from outside through a fundamental improvement in their economic position, such as she considered could not fail to result from her husband's growing fame. If only, she thought, there could be a relaxation of the incessant pressure, arising from this cause, which made itself felt more or less directly upon him too; if, instead of sacrificing half his time and strength to mere money-making, he were free to devote his undivided attention to his real vocation; and lastly, if his pleasures were to prove more wholesome to him, both physically and mentally, now that he no longer had to expend so much energy in pursuit of them, and could enjoy them with a far better conscience – then surely his whole condition must soon become easier and more natural and tranquil. She even considered a possible change of residence, for his marked preference for Vienna, where, however, in her opinion, no real good would come to him, might after all be overcome.

But for the first decisive step towards the realization of her ideas and wishes Madame Mozart looked to the success of the new opera with which their present journey was concerned.

The composition had now progressed well beyond the first half. Competent judges among his intimate friends who had watched the development of this remarkable work since its inception, and thus were certain to have an adequate grasp of its character and the means by which it achieved its effects, spoke of it everywhere in such terms that many, even of his adversaries, could feel sure that before six months were out this Don Giovanni would have convulsed the whole musical world of Germany from one end to the other, turned it topsy-turvy and taken it by storm. More cautious and guarded views were expressed in the sympathetic comments of those who, judging from the standpoint of contemporary music, scarcely hoped for a rapid and general success. The Master himself secretly shared their doubts, which proved only too well grounded.

For her part, as is always the way with women, who, once their feelings are deeply involved, and still further biased by the warmth of a perfectly just desire, will not allow themselves to be turned aside so often as men do by subsequent doubts arising out of this cause or that, Konstanze stood firmly by her conviction and had had occasion to take up the cudgels for it again just now in the carriage. She did so in her lively and exuberant way, with redoubled assiduity, for during the conversation described above, which, since it could in no way advance matters, had broken off in the most unsatisfactory way, Mozart's spirits had already drooped noticeably. She explained to her husband in great detail and with unclouded cheerfulness how, on their return home, she proposed to use the hundred ducats agreed upon by the manager of the Prague opera as the fee to be paid for the score, for meeting the most pressing items, and so forth, and further how, according to the budget she had drawn up, she hoped to get through the whole of the coming winter easily, up to the early spring.

'Your Herr Boldini will feather his nest well out of the opera, believe me; and if he is half the man of honour you always make him out to be, he will allow you a nice little extra percentage on the sums paid him one after the other by the opera-houses for their transcripts of the score; and even if he doesn't, well, God be praised, we have other chances in prospect besides, and a thousand times more solid ones, too. I have all sorts of notions in my head.'

'Out with them, then!'

'A little bird told me, not so long ago, that the King of Prussia was wanting a conductor.'

'Oho!'

'I mean, a general director of music. Let me indulge my fancy a bit! I inherit the weakness from my mother!'

'Go ahead, then! The wilder the better!'

'No, it will all be perfectly natural. To anticipate, then: supposing that a year from now——'

'When the Pope marries Mary Ann, I suppose?'

'Be quiet, Tom Fool! I repeat that by St Giles's day next year there must be no trace to be found high or low in Vienna of any court composer to His Imperial Majesty by the name of Wolf Mozart.'

'The deuce there mustn't!'

'I can already imagine how our old friends will be talking about us, and all the tales they will have to tell one another.'

'For example?'

'Well, this one, for instance: early one morning, after nine o'clock, our enthusiastic old Volkstett comes tacking across the Kohlmarkt at her most furious pace, prepared to take her friends' houses by storm. She has been away for three months, for the great visit to her brother-in-law in Saxony, her daily topic of conversation ever since we have known her, has at last taken place; she has been back since the night before, and now, with her heart full to overflowing – it is fit to burst with travellers' joy and friendly impatience and the most delicious tit-bits of news – off she goes like a shot to pour it all out to the Colonel's wife. Up the stairs she goes, and raps at the door without waiting for any "Come in!" Imagine the rapture and the mutual embraces! "Well, my best and dearest Mrs Colonel," she begins, taking breath after a few preliminary remarks, "I have brought you a whole budget of greetings – now guess from whom! I have not come quite, quite straight from Stendal, but went a little way round, towards the left, as far as Brandenburg." – "What! Is it possible? You got as far as Berlin – and called on the Mozarts?" "Ten heavenly days I spent there!" "Oh, my dear, my sweet, my incomparable Mrs. General, do tell me, do describe it! How are our dear young couple? Are they still as pleased with things there as they were at first? It is fabulous, unbelievable, that this very day – and even more so now that you have come straight from him. Mozart as a Berliner! How is he getting on? How does he look, now?" "Oh, Mozart! You should just see him! This summer the King sent him to Karlsbad. When would such an idea have occurred to his beloved Emperor Joseph, hey? The two of them were barely home again before I arrived. He is radiant with life and health, and as round and plump and lively as quick-silver. His eyes simply beam with happiness and comfort!'' '

And now, still keeping up her assumed rôle, the speaker began to paint their new position in the most rosy colours; from his apartment on Unter den Linden and his garden and villa to the brilliant scenes of his public activity and the intimate court circles in which he had to accompany the Queen at the piano, the picture she drew of it brought the whole thing before them as though it had been real and present. She improvised whole conversations and the most glorious anecdotes. She seemed positively more at home in the royal capital, at Potsdam and Sanssouci, than in the Palace of Schönbrunn and the Imperial Burg. Besides, she was sly enough to endow the person of our hero with a number of entirely novel domestic qualities which had developed on the solid foundation of his life in Prussia, and among which the above-mentioned Frau Volkstett, as the supreme marvel and proof of how extremes meet, had actually noted the beginnings of a slight touch of stinginess, which sat upon him delightfully.

'''Yes, only imagine it, he has his three thousand thalers coming in regularly, and for what? For giving a chamber concert in the royal apart-ments once a week and conducting the grand opera twice. Oh, Mrs Colonel, I saw him, our dear, precious little man, surrounded by his crack orchestra, trained by himself, which worships him! I sat with Frau Mozart in her box, immediately opposite the Royalties! And what was printed on the bills, if you please? I brought one away for you, with a little holiday present from me and the Mozarts wrapped up in it. Look here, now, only read it: there it stands printed in letters an ell high!'' ''Heaven help us! What? 'Tarar?' '' ''Yes! There now, my dear, the things one sees in life! Two years ago, when Mozart was writing 'Don Giovanni,' and that ac-cursed, venomous, sallow-faced Salieri was already scheming on the sly how he might repeat on his own territory the triumph he had carried off in Paris with his own piece, and let our good, snuff-loving public, still en-chanted with 'Cosa rara,' see, just for once in a way, what sort of a hawk he was, and he and his myrmidons were already colloguing and plotting how they might put 'Don Giovanni' on the stage in a nicely plucked condition, neither dead nor alive, as they had done with 'Figaro' before it – do you know, I vowed then and there that if the abominable piece were given, I would not go near it for anything on earth! And kept my word, too! While everybody was rushing to it as hard as they could go, and you among them, Mrs Colonel, I sat at home by my own stove, took my cat on my lap and ate my bit of tripe; and I did the same on the next two occasions as well. But now, only think of it, 'Tarar' on the stage at the Berlin opera-house, the work of his mortal enemy, conducted by Mozart! "You really must come!" he cried, within the very first quarter of an hour, "if only so that you can tell them in Vienna whether I have harmed a single hair of young Absalom's head. I only wish he had been there himself, so that the green-eyed monster might see that I have no need to make a botch of some other fellow's work only, after all, to remain exactly what I was before!"' '

'*Brava! bravissima!*' cried Mozart at the top of his voice, and taking his little wife by the ear, he covered her with kisses, fondled and toyed with her, so that her merry sport with the gay soap-bubbles of a dream future, which was never, alas! to be realized even to the most modest extent, dissolved in the end into sheer high spirits, laughter and frolic.

Meanwhile they had long since descended into the valley and were approaching a village which had already been conspicuous from the high ground, and close beyond which a small country mansion in the fashionable style, the seat of a certain Count Schinzberg, was visible in the smiling plain. It was here that they were to rest and bait the horses and have their midday meal. The inn at which they drew up stood by itself at the end of the village beside the highroad, from which a poplar avenue less than six hundred paces long branched off towards his lordship's garden.

When they had alighted, Mozart, as usual, left the ordering of dinner to his wife. Meanwhile he himself called for a glass of wine in the room downstairs, while she, after a drink of fresh water, asked no more than a quiet corner where she might take a short nap. She was shown upstairs and her husband followed, singing and whistling to himself in the best of spirits. In a clean, whitewashed room, which was quickly aired, among other old-fashioned pieces of furniture of more distinguished origin – for they had no doubt migrated there at some time or another from the bed-chambers of the Schloss – stood a neat, light bed with a painted tester supported on slender green-lacquered columns, its silken curtains long since replaced by more ordinary stuff. Konstanze settled down comfortably, he promised to wake her in good time, she bolted the door behind him, and he forthwith betook himself to the public bar in search of entertainment. But not a soul was there save the innkeeper, and since the conversation of the latter was as little to the visitor's liking as his wine, he said he would like to take a walk as far as the Schloss garden till dinner was ready. It was open to respectable strangers, he was told, and on that day, moreover, the family were away on an excursion.

He went out, and had soon covered the short distance from there to the metal-work gates, which were standing open; he then sauntered slowly along a tall avenue of ancient lime-trees, at the end of which, on the left, he suddenly found the façade of the mansion before him a short distance away. It was built in the Italian style, washed over with a light colour, and approached in front by a broad double flight of stone steps; the slate roof was adorned with a few statues of gods and goddesses in the conventional style then in vogue, together with a balustrade.

Issuing from between two large flower-beds, still rich with bloom, our Master walked towards the part of the grounds where the shrubberies were, passing by a few fine, sombre groups of pine-trees, and, following the twists and turns of the winding paths, gradually turned his steps back in the direction of the more open parts, towards the busy plash of a flowing fountain, at which he soon arrived.

The ample breadth of its oval basin was surrounded by a carefully tended group of orange-trees in tubs, interspersed with laurels and olean-ders; the whole was surrounded by a soft, sanded path, off which opened a small trellised bower. This arbour offered a most agreeable resting-place; a little table stood in front of the seat, and Mozart sat down at it towards the front, near the entrance.

His ears pleasantly beguiled by the plash of water, and his eyes resting

upon an orange-tree of moderate size, which stood on the ground apart
from the rest close by his side, thickly hung with the most beautiful fruit,
our friend was immediately carried back by this glimpse of the south to a
charming memory of his boyhood's days. With a pensive smile he reached
out towards the nearest orange, as though to try the feel of its splendid
roundness and juicy coolness in the hollow of his hand. But closely connected with that scene from his youth which had risen up again before him
was a long-effaced musical reminiscence, the faint trace of which he dreamily
pursued awhile. And now his eyes lit up and wandered about him, now
here, now there; he was seized by an idea, which he at once followed up
eagerly. Absent-mindedly he grasped the orange a second time; it came
away from the stalk, and lay there in his hand. He looked upon it, but saw
it not; so lost was he, indeed, in his artistic abstraction that, as he continued to turn the fragrant fruit over and over under his nose, humming
inaudibly between his lips now the beginning and now the end of a melody,
at last he instinctively drew an enamelled case from the side pocket of his
coat, took from it a small silver-handled knife, and slowly divided the
yellow, spherical mass from top to bottom. He may have been obscurely
prompted by a vague feeling of thirst, but his quickened senses were content to inhale the precious fragrance. For a whole minute he stared at the
two inner surfaces, gently put them together again, then took them apart
and fitted them together once more.

But now he heard footsteps close at hand; he started, and the consciousness of where he was and what he had been doing abruptly flashed upon
him. Though already in the act of concealing the orange, he paused,
whether out of pride or because it was too late. A big, broad-shouldered
man in livery stood before him, the Count's gardener. The man must,
moreover, have seen that last suspicious movement, and stood for a few
seconds in shocked silence. Mozart, equally speechless, and as though
riveted to his seat, fixed his blue eyes upon the man's face, blushing visibly,
yet with a sort of boldness and dignity; then he laid the apparently un-
damaged orange in the centre of the table – had any third person been

present, it would have been a highly comical sight – with a sort of defiant and spirited flourish.

'Beg pardon,' now began the gardener, in a covertly surly tone, having taken a good look at the stranger's not very prepossessing costume, 'I do not know whom I have the . . .'

'Kapellmeister Mozart from Vienna.'

'You are doubtless known to the family?

'I am a stranger here, travelling through. Is his lordship the Count at home?'

'No.'

'His lady, then?'

'She's engaged, and it's not easy to have a word with her.'

Mozart rose, and made as if to depart.

'By your leave, Sir, how comes it that you have helped yourself here like this?'

'What?' cried Mozart, 'helped myself? The devil! Do you suppose, fellow, that I meant to steal, and gobble the thing up?'

'Seeing is believing, Sir. These fruits have been counted, and I am responsible for them. The tree is intended by his lordship for a special occasion and is shortly to be removed. I don't let you go till I have reported the matter and you have proved to my satisfaction how this business happened.'

'Very well, then, I will wait here for the present. You may depend upon that.'

The gardener looked about him in some indecision, and Mozart, thinking it was, perhaps, only a matter of a tip, put his hand in his pocket, only to find that he had not so much as a copper about him.

Two under-gardeners now did, in fact, come up, lifted the tree on to a barrow and took it away. Meanwhile our Master had drawn out his wallet, taken from it a blank sheet of paper, and begun to write in pencil, the gardener still standing his ground.

'Most gracious lady, Here I sit in your paradise, though not one of the blest, like Adam of old after eating the apple. The calamity has happened, and I cannot even throw the blame on my good Eve, who at this very moment, with the Graces and Loves of a four-post bed sporting around her, is enjoying the most innocent slumber at the hotel. Command me, and I will answer in person to your ladyship for my act of sacrilege, inexplicable even to myself.

    'In sincere humiliation,

        'Your ladyship's most humble servant,

            'W. A. Mozart, on the way to Prague.'

He handed the somewhat clumsily folded note with the necessary instructions to the servant, who was waiting in painful uneasiness.

The marplot was no sooner gone than the roll of wheels was heard from the other side of the Schloss. It was the Count, escorting from the neighbouring estate a niece of his with her future husband, a rich young baron. Since the latter's mother had not left the house for years, the ceremony of betrothal had taken place that day in her presence. The occasion was now to be celebrated here, too, at another merry party among a few relations; for since her childhood the Schloss had been to Eugenie a second home, where she was like a daughter of the house. The Countess had driven home a little earlier with her son Max, the lieutenant, for the purpose of completing various arrangements. And now everyone in the Schloss might have been seen in a perfect commotion about the stairs and corridors, and it was only with difficulty that the gardener did at last succeed in handing her ladyship the note in the ante-room; she did not, however, open it on the spot, but without paying much attention to the messenger's words, went fussing off again. Servant after servant hurried past him, footmen, lady's maids, and valets; he asked for his lordship – but he was changing his clothes; he then went in search of Count Max, and found him in his room, but he was talking earnestly with the Baron, and cut the man short, as though afraid he was trying to tell him something or ask some question on a subject about which not a whisper must yet be heard. 'I'm just coming,' he said. 'Now be off.' It was some time before the father and son emerged simultaneously from their rooms and heard the disastrous news.

'It really is an infernal plague!' cried the stout, good-natured, but rather

peppery Count. 'It really passes all comprehension! A musician from Vienna, did you say? Some low fellow, I suppose, hanging round for a tip, and ready to pick up anything he can find at the same time?'

'By your lordship's leave, he does not look quite that sort. He seems to me not quite right in the head; besides, he is very high and mighty. Moser, he calls himself. He is waiting for your decision down there. I told Franz to hang about and keep an eye on him.'

'What the devil is the use of that now the harm is done? Even if I were to have the fool locked up, that would not repair the damage! I had told you a thousand times that the front gate should always be kept locked. This business would have been prevented, at any rate, if you had taken your measures in time.'

At this point the Countess came hurriedly out of the adjoining boudoir in a state of joyous excitement, holding the open letter in her hand. 'Do you know,' she exclaimed, 'who is down there? For Heaven's sake read the letter – Mozart, the composer from Vienna! Somebody must go at once and invite him up to the house. I am afraid he may already be gone. What will he think of me? You there, Velten, did you treat him politely? Now what was it that really happened?'

'Happened?' retorted her husband, whose irritation could not be altogether allayed on the spot by the prospect of a visit from a famous man, 'the crazy fellow has picked one of the nine oranges from the tree I had intended for Eugenie. The – the – monster! And so the whole point of our little pleasantry is gone, and Max might just as well tear up his poem.'

'Oh no!' insisted the lady, 'the deficiency can easily be made good. Only leave it to me. Now go, both of you, set the good man at liberty and welcome him in the kindest and most complimentary fashion you possibly can. If we can devise any way of keeping him, he shall go no further to-day. If you do not find him still in the garden, go and look for him at the inn and bring him here with his wife. Chance could have brought us no finer gift or lovelier surprise for Eugenie on such an occasion.'

'Of course!' replied Max, 'that was my own first thought, too. Come, Papa, quick! And,' he added, as they ran swiftly down the stairs, 'you may set your mind at rest about the verses. The ninth Muse shall not go short; on the contrary, I shall manage to turn this mishap to special advantage.' 'Impossible!' 'Yes I shall, really and truly.' 'Well, if that is so – mind, I am taking your word for it – we will do the crazy fellow every imaginable honour.'

While this was taking place in the Schloss our hero, though virtually a prisoner, had his mind reasonably at rest with regard to the upshot of the affair, and occupied himself for a considerable time in writing. But when nobody at all appeared, he began pacing restlessly to and fro, during which time an urgent message arrived from the inn to say that dinner was long since ready, and would he kindly come at once, for the postillion was urging haste. He was therefore trying to gather up his belongings and meant to start without delay, when the two gentlemen appeared before the arbour.

The Count greeted him jovially in his powerful ringing voice, almost like an old acquaintance, and gave him no time to make excuses, but at once expressed his desire to entertain both husband and wife in his family circle, at least for that afternoon and evening. 'You are so little of a stranger to us, my dearest Maestro, that scarcely anywhere else, I venture to say, is the name of Mozart mentioned more often, or with greater enthusiasm than here. My niece sings and plays, she spends almost the whole day at the grand piano, she knows your works by heart, and is most anxious to have the chance of seeing you at closer quarters than was possible at one of your concerts last winter. And since we are shortly going to Vienna for a few weeks, relations had promised us an invitation to the house of Prince Galitzin, where you are fairly often to be found. But now you are off to Prague, and will not be back for some time, and goodness knows whether you will come this way on your return journey! Do take a holiday for to-day and to-morrow! We will send your conveyance home at once, and you must allow me to make arrangements for the rest of your journey.'

The composer, who on such occasions as this, when friendship or enjoyment was concerned, would readily have sacrificed ten times more than was asked of him now, did not take long to think it over; he joyfully conceded this one half day, but, he said, on the morrow they must proceed upon their way as early as possible. Count Max begged that he might have the pleasure of fetching Madame Mozart and making all necessary arrangements at the inn. He went off, and a carriage was to follow him immediately.

As to this young man, we may remark in passing that with the sunny temperament inherited from his father and mother, he combined talent and a love of fine literature, and, though conscious of no real vocation for the military profession, had none the less distinguished himself as an officer by his intelligence and good conduct. He had a knowledge of French literature, and at that time, when German verse was held in but small esteem in high society, had won praise and favour by the quite uncommon ease with which he handled the poetic form in his mother tongue, following

such good models as he found in Hagedorn, Götz and others. On this particular day, as we have already gathered, an especially gratifying occasion
had offered itself for the exercise of his talent.

He found Madame Mozart gossiping with the innkeeper's daughter at
the ready-laid table, where she had already started upon a plate of soup.
She was too well used to extraordinary happenings and audacious pranks
on the part of her husband to be more than mildly perturbed at the appear-
ance of the young officer and the mission entrusted to him. With unruffled
good-temper and in cool, practical fashion she settled matters then and
there and gave all requisite orders in person. The luggage was repacked,
the bill paid, the postillion dismissed, she got ready without any undue fuss
over her toilette, and drove off cheerfully to the Schloss with her escort,
never suspecting in how strange a fashion her husband had gained an
entrance there.

Meanwhile he was already installed most comfortably and excellently
entertained. After a time he saw Eugenie, a blooming creature of great charm
and depth of feeling, with her affianced lover. She was golden-haired, her
slender form festally attired in lustrous crimson silk with costly laces, and
round her brow was a white fillet adorned with orient pearls. The Baron,
but little older than herself, with a gentle, candid nature, seemed in every
respect worthy of her.

The first brunt of the conversation was borne, if anything too bountifully,
by the kindly, whimsical host, thanks to his rather exuberant way of talking, abundantly embellished with jests and anecdotes. Refreshments were
handed round, of which our traveller was by no means chary.

Somebody had opened the pianoforte, *The Marriage of Figaro* stood
open on the rack, and the young lady, accompanied by the Baron, made
ready to sing Susanna's aria in the garden-scene, from which we inhale in
great streams the very spirit of tender passion, like the aromatic breezes
of the summer night. The delicate flush on Eugenie's cheek changed for a
breathing-space to an extreme pallor; but with the first full note that passed
her lips she found relief from the sense of oppression which had seemed to
constrict her bosom. Smiling and confident, she rode, as it were, on the

crest of the wave, and the savour of this moment, unique, perhaps, in its way, among all the days of her life, filled her with a corresponding exaltation.

Mozart was clearly surprised. When she had finished, he went up to her and, in his simple way, speaking straight from the heart, began as follows: 'What is a man to say, dear child, in a case like that of the blessed sunshine, whose best praise is that everyone straightway feels well in its presence! During such singing as this the soul feels like a baby in its bath; it laughs and wonders, and can think of nothing better in the world. Then too, believe me, it is not every day that the likes of us in Vienna have the chance of listening to our very selves, so pure, so unadorned and warm – in short, so complete.' And with these words he took her hand and kissed it with all his heart. The noble kindliness of the man and his goodness of heart, no less than the handsome tribute with which he had honoured her talent, filled Eugenie with that overmastering emotion that is like a touch of vertigo, and her eyes must needs fill suddenly with tears.

At this point Madame Mozart entered the room, and close upon her appeared some other guests who were expected – a baron's family from the neighbourhood, closely related to that of the Count and with a daughter, Franziska, who had been attached since childhood to the future bride by ties of the most tender affection, and felt quite at home in the house.

They all exchanged greetings, embraces and congratulations, the two visitors from Vienna were introduced, and Mozart seated himself at the grand piano. He played a movement from a concerto of his own composition, which Eugenie was practising at the time.

The effect of such a performance in so small a party as this naturally differs from one in a public place by reason of the infinite satisfaction to be drawn from direct contact with the person and genius of the artist within the familiar walls of home.

It was one of those brilliant pieces in which, as though by some caprice, pure beauty elects of its own free will to place itself at the command of elegance, but in such a way as only, so to speak, to veil itself in this more wanton play of forms, dissembling itself behind a host of brilliant lights, yet betraying in its every movement its essential nobility, and pouring forth lavishly a splendid fulness of passion.

The Countess observed to herself that the majority of the audience, perhaps not excepting even Eugenie herself, for all their rapt attention and awed silence during this magical playing, were none the less greatly torn between the claims of eye and ear. As, in spite of themselves, they watched the composer, with the simple, almost stiff carriage of his body, his good-humoured face and the circling action of his small hands, it was certainly far from easy to stem the inrush of a thousand jostling ideas on the subject of this man of wonder.

Turning towards Madame Mozart when the Master had risen from the piano, the Count remarked: 'When faced with an artist of renown, for whom one feels it incumbent upon one to turn some apt and knowledgeable compliment – which is not everybody's knack, I may say – how fortunate are kings and emperors! From such lips as theirs every remark seems original and out of the common. There is nothing they may not venture to say; and how nice and easy it is to stand just behind your husband's chair, and, on the closing chord of some brilliant improvisation, to tap this modest, tip-top performer on the shoulder and say: "You are a devil of a fellow, my dear Mozart!" No sooner is the word out of his lips than it flies round the room like wild-fire: "What was it he said to him?" "A devil of a fellow, he called him!" And every soul who fiddles or pipes or composes is wild with rage at this one word; in short, that is your grand style, the familiar style of emperors, the inimitable style which I have always envied your Josefs and Friedrichs, and never more than at present, when I am simply in despair because I cannot discover a doit of any wit superior to that in my pockets.'

The way in which the droll old fellow brought this out was irresistible for all its bluntness, and could not fail to raise a laugh.

But now, at their hostess's bidding, the company made a move towards the round dining-parlour, which had been decorated for the occasion, so that as they entered the festal perfume of flowers floated out to meet them, with a cooler air propitious to the appetite.

Each took the place tactfully assigned to him, the distinguished visitor, for his part, being placed opposite the betrothed couple. On one side he had a little elderly lady, a maiden aunt of Franziska's, and his neighbour on the other side was the fascinating young niece herself, who soon managed to commend herself to his especial approbation by her intelligence and liveliness. Frau Konstanze sat between the master of the house and her amiable escort the lieutenant. The rest fell into place, and so they sat down to table eleven in all, each lady, so far as possible, next a gentleman, while the lower end was left empty. In the middle rose two huge great porcelain centre-pieces with painted figures bearing on their heads ample dishes piled high with natural flowers and fruit. Round the walls of the room hung rich garlands. Everything else that was in the room, or was brought into it in constant succession, seemed to announce a prolonged revel. Partly on the table among the dishes and plates, partly on the sideboard in the background, there gleamed every variety of noble wine, from a red that was almost black to the yellow-tinged white whose foaming gaiety is traditionally reserved to crown the second half of a feast.

Till this point had nearly arrived the conversation had ranged over every sort of topic, being kept up by several parties with equal animation. But from the very first the Count had thrown out an occasional distant allusion to Mozart's adventure in the garden, and his references now became more and more mischievous and pointed, till some smiled mysteriously, while the others vainly racked their brains to discover what he could possibly mean, till at last our friend spoke up as follows:

'In Heaven's name!' he began, 'I am ready to confess exactly how it was that I had the honour of becoming acquainted with this noble house. I do not play a particularly dignified rôle in the story, and instead of sitting here enjoying myself at table, it was touch and go that I did not find myself under arrest in some remote corner of this lordly mansion, where I might have sat with an empty stomach staring at the spiders' webs on the walls.'

'There!' cried Madame Mozart, 'now I shall hear a pretty story!'

He then described in detail first how he had left his wife at the White Horse, then his walk in the park, his ill-starred adventure in the arbour, his

encounter with the custodians of order in the garden, in short, very much
what we already know, all of which revelations were made with the utmost
candour and to the high delight of his listeners. It seemed as though the
laughter would never come to an end; even the self-possessed Eugenie
could not help herself, but fairly shook with it.

'Well,' he went on, 'the proverb says that he who has the profit can face
the laughter. And I have turned a little profit of my own out of the adventure, as you soon shall see. But first of all you must hear how it really came
about that my old childish head managed so to forget itself. A memory of
my youth had something to do with it.

'In the spring of 1770, as a lad of thirteen, I went with my father on a tour
in Italy. We travelled from Rome to Naples. I had played twice at the Con-
servatorio and on various occasions elsewhere too. The nobility and clergy
paid us many kind attentions, and one *abbate* attached himself to us in
particular who plumed himself upon his discriminating taste and had,
moreover, a certain influence at court. The day before we left he drove us,
in company with a few other gentlemen, to one of the royal gardens, that
of the Villa Reale, beside the magnificent road that runs along next the
sea, where a troupe of Sicilian *commedianti* was performing – *figli di Net-
tuno*, sons of Neptune, as they called themselves among other high-sounding
titles. We sat in a large and distinguished audience, among which was the
charming young Queen Carolina herself, with two princesses, on a long
row of seats shaded by a low gallery with a tent-like awning, along the wall
of which the waves murmured below. The sea, streaked with changing hues,
reflected in a blaze of glory the blue and sunny skies above. Immediately
opposite was Vesuvius, and on our left a lovely coast lay glimmering in a
soft curve.

'The first part of the entertainment was over: it had been performed on
the dry planks of a sort of raft floating on the water, and had nothing very
remarkable about it; but the second and finer half was entirely made up
of feats of boating, swimming and diving, and has always remained with all
its details freshly imprinted upon my memory.

'From the far side of the raft two graceful, very lightly built barks approached and drew together, both bound, as it seemed, on a pleasure-cruise. One, a trifle the larger, was furnished with a half-deck, and equipped, next the rowers' benches, with a slender mast and sail; it was gorgeously painted besides and had a gilded prow. Five young men of ideal beauty, scantily clad and with arms, breast and legs seemingly bare, now busied themselves at the helm, now sported with their lady-loves, an equal number of pretty girls. One of these, who was seated in the middle of the deck weaving garlands of flowers, stood out among all the rest by her stature and beauty as well as her adornments. They waited on her willingly, spread an awning over her to keep off the sun, and handed her the flowers out of the basket. A girl with a flute sat at her feet, accompanying the songs of the others with its limpid notes. Nor did this surpassing beauty lack her own special protector; yet the couple bore themselves toward each other with some indifference, and the lover, it almost seemed to me, was a trifle uncouth.

'Meanwhile the other and simpler craft had drawn closer. In it could be seen none but young men. The youths in the first boat wore a vivid red, and the second band, in like fashion, were dressed in sea-green. They started at the sight of the charming girls, waved greetings to them, and showed a desire to be better acquainted. Thereupon the liveliest of the maidens took a rose from her bosom and held it roguishly on high, as though enquiring whether such gifts would be acceptable, to which answer came back from all sides in unequivocal gestures. The reds looked on in gloomy disdain, but could do nothing when several of the maidens agreed that they would at least throw the poor fellows something to relieve their hunger and thirst. There was a basket of oranges standing on deck – though most likely they were only yellow balls made to resemble the fruit. And now began an enchanting scene accompanied by the orchestra, which was posted on the sea-wall.

'One of the maidens opened fire, being the first to toss a few oranges deftly across, which were caught with equal skill and immediately returned; to and fro they went, and soon, as more and more of the girls joined in, oranges by the dozen were flying back and forth at an ever-increasing speed. The beauty amidships took no part in the fray, beyond looking on from her stool with intense curiosity. We could not wonder enough at the skill displayed by both sides. The coats circled slowly round and round each other at a distance of some thirty paces, now lying broadside on, now at an angle, one being half across the other's bows; there were some four-and-twenty balls constantly in the air, yet such was the medley that one believed one saw many more. At times a regular cross-fire would spring up, while then again they would rise and fall in a lofty curve, scarce one missing its aim on either side. It was as though they fell of their own accord into the fingers opened to catch them, as though drawn by some compelling force.

'Yet agreeably though the eye was engaged, the melodies accompanied them full as sweetly to the ear: Sicilian airs, dances, *saltarelli*, *canzoni a ballo*, a whole miscellany, strung lightly together like a garland. The youthful princess, a sweet, ingenuous creature of about my own age, nodded her head so prettily in time to the music. I can still see before me to-day her smile and the long lashes fringing her eyes.

'Now let me describe shortly the rest of the merry scene, though it has no further bearing on the point of interest to me. It would be hard to imagine anything prettier. As the skirmish gradually died down, and only a few missiles were now still exchanged, while the girls collected their golden apples and returned them to the basket, a boy over yonder, as though in play, had picked up an ample green-meshed net and held it for a time under water; he drew it in, and to the astonishment of all a great fish was to be seen in it, gleaming with azure, green and gold. Those nearest him were springing eagerly forward to pull it out, when it slipped from their hands, as though alive, and fell into the sea. But this was only a ruse arranged in order to mislead the reds and tempt them from their boat. And sure enough, as though bewitched by this marvel, they no sooner noticed that the creature would not sink, but remained playing on the surface, than, without a moment's hesitation, they all hurled themselves into the sea, and the greens likewise, till we saw twelve expert and finely-built swimmers endeavouring to catch the elusive fish as it bobbed about on the waves, at

times disappearing beneath them for minutes on end, only to appear again now here, now there, between the legs of one or the breast and chin of another. All of a sudden, while the reds were hottest in pursuit of their quarry, the other party saw its chance, and, quick as lightning, boarded the other boat, now entirely abandoned to the maidens, amid a hubbub of screams from the latter. The most nobly-proportioned of the youths, built like a Mercury, with his face lit up with joy, rushed towards the loveliest maiden of them all, clasped her in his arms and kissed her, while, far from joining in the screams of the others, she threw her arms round the young man with equal ardour, for she knew him well. The crew that had been tricked swam hastily to the spot, but were driven off by those on board with oars and weapons. Their baffled rage, the frightened screams of the girls, the vehement resistance of a few of them, their prayers and supplications, almost drowned the music, which had suddenly assumed a different character. It was lovely beyond description, and the audience broke into a storm of enthusiasm.

'At this moment the sail, which till then had been loosely brailed up, was lowered: out of it stepped a rosy boy with silver wings, a bow and arrows and a quiver, and poised lightly on the bowsprit in a graceful attitude. By this time the oars were all hard at work, and the sail swelled, but, mightier than either, the presence of the god and the rushing forward sweep of his pose seemed to drive the craft onward so fast that the swimmers in almost breathless pursuit, one holding the golden fish in his left hand high above his head, soon gave up hope, and, their strength being now exhausted, were forced to seek refuge in the boat that had been abandoned. Meanwhile the greens had reached a small bush-grown peninsula, where a splendid boat appeared unexpectedly in ambush, full of armed comrades. Faced with such a threatening situation the little band ran up a white flag as a sign that they desired an amicable parley. Encouraged by a like signal from the other side, they rowed on towards that stopping-place, and soon we saw all the nice girls save the one, who willingly remained behind, climb merrily on board their own ship together with their lovers. And with this the comedy was at an end.'

'It seems to me,' whispered Eugenie to the Baron with shining eyes during a pause in which everybody was loud in praise of what they had just heard, 'that we have just had, as it were, a symphonic picture painted from beginning to end, and, what is more, a perfect portrayal of Mozart's own spirit in all its gaiety. Am I not right? Is not the whole charm of 'Figaro' to be found in it?'

Her affianced lover was on the point of repeating her remark to the composer, when the latter went on to say: 'It is now seventeen years since I saw Italy. Who that has once seen it, and especially Naples, does not think about it for the rest of his life, even if, like me, he had but half grown out of his childhood's garments? But never did that last lovely evening on the Gulf rise up again before my mind so vividly as to-day in your garden. If I closed my eyes, the whole scene lay stretched before me, perfectly clear, bright and distinct, with the last veil of haze floating up from it into the air. Sea and shore, mountain and city, the bright-hued throng moving along the water's edge, and then the wondrous play of the criss-crossing balls! I thought the selfsame music still sounded in my ears, a whole rose-garland of joyous melodies floated through my head, my own and other people's, a perfect Babel, one for ever succeeding the other. A little dance-tune tripped out inconsequently in six-eight time, completely new to me. "Stop!" I thought, "What have we here? That seems a devilish pretty thing!" I looked closer – "Heavens!" I cried, "why, there is Masetto, there is Zerlina!" ' He laughed across at Madame Mozart, who at once guessed his meaning.

'The point,' he continued, 'is simply this: in my first act there was one little light number still unwritten, a duet and chorus for a rustic wedding. For two months ago, when I tried to deal with this number in its proper order, the right thing simply refused to come at the first attempt. A simple childlike tune, bubbling over and over with merriment, a knot of fresh flowers with fluttering ribbons worn at the maiden's breast – that is what it should have been. But since one must not force anything, even in the smallest detail, and since trifles of that sort often write themselves of their own accord as one goes along, I just passed it by, and in the progress of my more important work gave it scarcely another thought. To-day in the carriage, shortly before we drove into the village, the words fleeted swiftly through my mind; but at the moment nothing more came of it – at least, not to my knowledge. Very well! About an hour later, in the arbour by the fountain, I got hold of a motive, better and more apt than any I could have invented at any other time or in any other way. Art brings one odd experiences at times, but no such trick was ever played on me before. For a tune fitting the verses absolutely like a glove – but there, I must not anticipate, we have not got to that point yet; the bird had still no more than poked its head out of the shell, so I set to work on the spot to get it out complete and perfect. All the time Zerlina's dance floated vividly before my eyes, and the smiling landscape of the Gulf of Naples blended mysteriously with it all. I heard the answering voices of bridegroom and bride, and the lads and lasses in chorus.'

And here Mozart trolled forth most merrily the opening bars of the ditty:

> 'Giovinette, che fate all'amore,
> Non lasciate che passi l'età.
> Se nel seno vi bulica il core
> Il remedio vedetelo quà. La-la-la! La-la-la! La-la-la!
> Che piacer, che piacer ci sarà. La-la-la-le-ra!'[1]

'Meanwhile my hands had wrought the monstrous mischief. Already Nemesis was hovering behind the bushes, and now stepped forth in the shape of this fearsome fellow in the blue braided uniform. Had a real eruption of Vesuvius, on that god-like evening, suddenly poured down a rain of black ashes, blotting out both audience and actors and all the glory of Parthenope, good Heavens, the catastrophe could not have been more un-

---

[1]The English words in Boosey's edition of *Don Giovanni* are as follows:
> 'Pretty maidens, it lies in your power,
> With the summer of life still in bloom,
> To preserve in each bosom life's flower,
> And be cheered by its dainty perfume. Tra! la la! etc.
> For then all will a sunshine assume. Lalalalera!'

The sentiment of the Italian words bears more resemblance to that of 'Gather ye roses while ye may.'

foreseen or horrible. A regular devil, he was! Scarcely ever has a man made me turn so hot all over. A face as of bronze – rather resembling Tiberius, the cruel Roman emperor. ''If that is what the servant looks like,'' I thought to myself when he had gone, ''what ever sort of face is his lordship likely to have!'' Yet, to tell the truth, I already counted a little bit on the protection of the ladies, and not without reason. For my Stanzerl there, my little wife, being a thought inquisitive by nature, had made the fat body at the inn tell her in my presence everything most worth knowing about all the persons composing this noble household; I was just standing by, and so I heard——'

At this point Madame Mozart could not refrain from interrupting him and assuring the company in the most circumstantial way that, on the contrary, it had been he who had asked the questions; whereupon a lively altercation sprang up between husband and wife, which gave rise to much laughter. 'Well, be that as it may,' he said, 'the long and short of it is that I heard something vaguely about a charming foster-daughter, who was engaged to be married and very lovely, and, what is more goodness itself and sang like an angel. ''*Per Dio!*'' the idea flashed across my mind, ''that will help you out of your scrape! You will just sit down exactly where you are, write out the little song as far as you can, explain your indiscretion precisely as it happened, and the whole thing will be a capital joke!'' No sooner said than done. I had time and to spare, and another nice clean bit of green-lined paper was forthcoming – and here is the result! I place it in these fair hands as an impromptu nuptial song, if you will accept it as such.'

Thus speaking he offered Eugenie across the table his most neatly written page of music, but her uncle's hand was quicker than hers, and he whisked it away, exclaiming: 'Patience one instant longer, my child!'

At a sign from him the folding-doors of the drawing-room were thrown open wide and some men-servants appeared, bearing into the room the fateful orange-tree noiselessly and decorously, and set it down on a bench at the lower end of the table; at the same time two slender myrtle-bushes were placed to right and left of it. An inscription attached to the stem of the orange-tree declared it to be the property of the future bride; but in front of it, on a bed of moss, lay a china plate covered with a napkin, revealing, when the cloth was removed, a halved orange, by the side of which her uncle, with a sly glance, laid the Master's autograph manuscript. The whole company broke forth at once into applause that would not end.

'I do believe,' said the Countess, 'that Eugenie has no idea yet what it is that stands before her. She really does not know her old favourite again in its new adornment of flowers and fruit.'

Puzzled and incredulous, the young lady looked now at the tree, now at her uncle. 'It is not possible,' she said. 'I know quite well that it was past saving.'

'So you think,' rejoined the latter, 'that all we have done has been to look for some sort of substitute? That would have been a nice thing to do! No! Only look here! I must do as the custom is in plays, when the son or brother who had been supposed dead proves his identity by his birth-marks and scars. Look here at this excrescence! And here again, the wrinkle running crosswise; you must have noticed it a hundred times. Well, is it the same, or is it not?' She could doubt it no longer; her amazement, emotion and joy were beyond description.

This tree was associated in the minds of the family with the more than century-old memory of a distinguished woman who is well worthy to be recalled here in a few words.

The uncle's grandfather, who had won a high reputation with the government at Vienna through his services to diplomacy and had been honoured with like confidence by two consecutive sovereigns, was equally fortunate in his own home on account of his remarkable wife, Renate Leonore. Her repeated visits to France had brought her into frequent contact with the brilliant court of Louis XIV and the most important men and women of that notable epoch. For all her frank participation in that unceasing round of the most intelligent pleasures of life, in no way, whether by deed or by word, did she belie her inborn German sense of honour and strict morality, of which the strongly marked features of the Countess's portrait, still in existence, bear the unmistakable impress. Thanks, indeed, to this disposition, she took up a characteristic attitude of candid

opposition in that society, and the correspondence she left behind her shows many a trace of the candour and vigorously combative spirit with which this original woman was capable of defending her sound principles and views, whether on matters of faith, literature, politics or anything else, and of attacking the defects of society without making herself in the slightest degree obnoxious to it. Her lively interest in all those to be met at the house of such a woman as Ninon, that true centre of the subtlest intellectual culture, was accordingly of such a character, and so regulated by these principles, as to be perfectly compatible with the loftier bonds of friendship that united her with one of the noblest ladies of that period, Madame de Sévigné. In addition to a number of sportive epigrams addressed to her by Chapelle, scribbled on the spur of the moment by the poet's hand on sheets of paper bordered with silver flowers, there were discovered in an ebony casket belonging to their grandmother after her death the most affectionate letters from the Marquise and her daughter to their outspoken friend in Austria.

It was, then, Madame de Sévigné from whose hand she had received one day on the terrace in the garden, during a fête at the Trianon, an orange-twig in bloom, which she had forthwith planted in a pot on chance and, since it fortunately struck root, had taken back with her to Germany.

For full twenty-five years the little tree grew steadily beneath her eye, and was afterwards tended by her children and grandchildren with the utmost solicitude. Apart from the personal value attaching to it, it might further be regarded as a living symbol of the subtle intellectual charm inherent in that age, which was considered almost divine, though nowadays, of course, we find little in it that is truly praiseworthy, for it already bore within it the germ of a sinister future, the world-shaking onset of which was even then not so very remote from the time of our innocent narrative.

It was Eugenie who had shown the most loving devotion to this heirloom handed down from her august ancestress, and for this reason her uncle had frequently remarked that it ought sooner or later to be handed over to her keeping. It was therefore all the more painful to the young lady when, in the spring of the previous year, which she had not spent at the Schloss, the tree began to droop, the leaves turned yellow, and several of its branches died. Since no especial reason could be discovered for its decay, and no remedy was of the least avail, the gardener soon gave it up for lost, though in the natural order of things it might easily have grown to twice or three times the age. The Count, however, advised by a neighbour who had special knowledge of such things, gave orders that, in accordance with a curious, and almost oracular recipe, such as is frequent among country-people, it should be secretly tended in a place apart, and his hope that he might one day surprise his beloved niece with the sight of her old friend, restored to fresh strength and perfect fruitfulness, was rewarded beyond all expectation. Restraining his impatience, and not without some anxiety as to whether the fruit, some of which had lately reached an advanced state of ripeness, would really hang so long upon the branch, he postponed the happy surprise for some weeks till that day's festivities, and no further words are needed to describe what must have been the kind-hearted old nobleman's feeling when he saw such a pleasure destroyed for him at the very last moment by a stranger.

Even before the meal the lieutenant had found time and opportunity to revise the poem that was to be his contribution to the solemn ceremony of presentation, and as best he could to adapt to the circumstances the otherwise rather too serious spirit of his verses by altering the ending. He now produced his sheet of paper, and, rising from his chair and turning towards his cousin, read out the poem. The purport of his stanzas was briefly as follows:

This scion of the much-vaunted Tree of the Hesperides, sprung from the soil of a western island ages ago in the garden of Juno as her wedding-gift from Mother Earth, and guarded by the three tuneful nymphs, had always hoped and longed for a like destiny, since the custom of presenting a lovely girl with a plant on her betrothal had long since descended from among the gods and become current among mortals.

After long and fruitless waiting it seemed at last that a maiden had been found to whom it might look in expectation. She showed herself well-disposed towards it, and often lingered at its side. But the laurel of the Muses,

standing proudly beside it on the fountain's verge, stung it to jealousy by
the threat of depriving this beauty, with her talent for the arts, of all heart
or sensibility to the love of men. In vain did the myrtle console it and teach
it patience by its own example; in the end it was the continued absence of
the loved one that aggravated its misery, and, after a short period of wast-
ing sickness, at last proved fatal.

Summer brings her home from afar, and with a happy change of heart.
Village, Schloss and garden all receive her with a thousand tokens of delight. Roses and lilies, their lustre now enhanced, gaze up at her in rapture,
though abashed. Shrubs and trees wave their branches to wish her happiness; but for one – and that, alas! the noblest – she comes too late. She
finds its crown withered, her fingers touch the lifeless stem and the crackling
tips of its branches. No more does it either know or see her who once had
tended it. What tears, what floods of tender lamentation does she now pour
forth!

But Apollo hears from afar the voice of his daughter. He comes, he
approaches, and looks with compassion upon her grief. At once he lays his
healing hands upon the tree, till it trembles, its dried-up sap surges mightily
within its bark, already young leaves sprout forth, already white blossoms
open here and there in ambrosial profusion. Yea – for what is impossible
to the celestial powers? – the fine globed fruits begin to swell, three times
three, to match the sisters nine; they grow and grow, their infant green
changing as we watch it to a golden hue. 'Phœbus – ' so the poem concluded –

> 'Phœbus reckons up the pieces,
> Counting them with loving care;
> And his mouth begins to water
> At the thought of what is there.
> Smilingly the god of music
> Plucks one, rich with juicy pride:
> Let us share it, gracious fair one,
> And for Amor's sake – divide!'

The poet received his meed of tumultuous applause, and the company
willingly forgave the grotesque *dénouement* by which the effect of the whole
poem, which had real feeling in it, was so completely destroyed.

Franziska, whose lively mother-wit had already been roused more than once, whether by the master of the house or by Mozart, now ran swiftly off, as though suddenly reminded of something, and returned with a dis-coloured English engraving of very large proportions, framed and glazed, which had been hanging almost disregarded in quite an out-of-the-way corner.

'So what I have always been told must be true,' she cried, propping up the picture at the end of the table, 'and there is nothing new under the sun! Here is a scene from the golden age – and have we not been living through it to-day? I hope, however, that Apollo will recognise himself in such a position.'

'Capital!' cried Max in triumph, 'and so all the time we really had him there, the handsome god, just bending meditatively over the sacred fount. Nor is that all – only see, there is an old satyr watching him from behind the bushes! One could almost swear that Apollo is trying to recall a long-forgotten Arcadian dance, which old Chiron taught him to play on the zither as a child!'

'So it is! It can be nothing else!' applauded Franziska, who was standing behind Mozart; 'and,' she continued, 'don't you see the branch laden with fruit drooping down towards the god?'

'Quite right; it is his sacred plant, the olive-tree.'

'Not at all! They are the most lovely oranges! Soon, in a fit of abstrac-tion, he will be stretching out his hand for one.'

'Nay!' cried Mozart, 'rather will he stop these mischievous lips with a thousand kisses.' And with these words he caught her by the arm and vowed not to let her go till she had yielded him her lips, which she did thereupon without very great resistance.

'But do tell us, Max,' said the Countess, 'what is that underneath the picture?'

'It is some verses from a famous ode of Horace. Not long ago the poet Ramler of Berlin translated the piece into German incomparably well. The rhythm of it is splendid. How glorious is this passage, for instance:

'. . . . et
Nunquam humeris positurus arcum,
Qui rore puro Castaliae lavit
Crines solutos, qui Lyciae tenet
Dumeta natalemque silvam,
Delius et Patareus Apollo.'[1]

'That is fine! Really fine!' said the Count, 'only here and there it re-
quires a little elucidation. Thus, for instance, ''he, whose bow is never laid
aside,'' would of course mean ''he who has always been the most assidu-
ous of fiddlers.'' But I am bound to say, my dear Mozart, you are sowing
discord between two loving hearts.'

'Indeed, I hope not. How so?'

'Eugenie is envious of her friend, and with very good reason, too.'

'Aha! You have already noted my weakness. But what says the future
husband?'

'Well, just for once or twice – I will look the other way.'

'Very good. We will profit by the opportunity. Meanwhile, never fear,
my lord. There is no danger, so long as the god here does not lend me his
face and long yellow locks. I only wish he would! He might take in exchange, here and now, Mozart's queue, and his best bit of ribbon too.'

[1] Horace, *Odes*, III, v. Ramler's translation, quoted by Mörike, is as follows:

'. . . hier, det auf der Schulter
Keinen untätigen Bogen führet!
Der seines Delos grünenden Mutterhain
Und Pataras beschatteten Strand bewohnt,
Der seines Hauptes goldne Locken
In die kastalischen Fluten tauchet.'

An English rendering of these verses by J. Howard Deazeley runs as follows:

. . . And he whose bow is never laid
Aside, who in Castalia's holy spring
His long locks laves, o'e Lycia's thickets king,
And o'er his native sward,
Of Patara and Delos lord.'

(From *Translations of the Odes of Horace into English Verse*, ed. M. Jourdain,
Messrs. J. M. Dent & Son's Temple Classics, by kind permission of the publishers.)

'But then,' laughed Franziska, 'Apollo would have to be careful how he went about laving his new French coiffure in Castalia's holy spring.'

Amid these jests and others of the kind the fun and mischief rose higher and higher. The wine was gradually having its effect upon the men; a number of healths were drunk, and Mozart became so much uplifted that, as his habit was, he broke into verse, in which the lieutenant kept his end up bravely, too, and even his Papa refused to be out of it, one or two of his efforts being wonderfully happy. But such things are too fleeting to be permanently captured for the purpose of our story; they refuse to lend themselves to repetition, for the very qualities that make them irresistible at the time, the general elation and the sparkle and joviality of personal expression, are lacking in both word and glance.

Among other toasts, the health of the Master was proposed by the old maiden lady, who promised him a whole long series of immortal works yet. '*A la bonne heure!* I am perfectly ready,' cried Mozart, clinking his wine-glass vigorously with hers. And now the Count struck up a song in his powerful and true intonation, improvising as his inspiration dictated:

The Count:
> May the gods grant inspiration
> For future works of your creation –

Max (continuing):
> But no Schikaneder, nor
> The Da Ponte any more –

Mozart:
> No, by God, I know they're bad,
> But what better's to be had?

The Count:
> And it is my earnest prayer
> That our Signor Bonbonnière,[1]
> That accurst Italian cheat,
> Lives to see them all complete!

Max:
> So let him live a hundred years –

Mozart:
> Unless, along with all his wares –

All three, *con forza:*
> Away the devil does not bear
> Our Signor Bonbonnière.

[1] This was Mozart's nickname for the Kapellmeister Salieri.

The Count was so uncommonly fond of singing that the trio thus casually begun developed, by the repetition of the last four lines, into what is known as a *'canon finitus'* [ending in a coda], and the maiden aunt had humour – or perhaps assurance – enough to embellish her worn soprano in the most capable fashion with all manner of roulades. Mozart then pledged his word that, when he had leisure enough, he would work out this lively trifle expressly for the company in accordance with the correct rules of composition, a promise which he afterwards fulfilled when back in Vienna.

Eugenie had for some time been quietly conning over her treasure from the bower of Tiberius, and now a general desire was voiced to hear the duet sung by her and the composer, while her uncle was glad to show off his voice once more in the chorus. So they rose from table and hastened to the piano in the large adjoining apartment.

Pure as was the delight with which this exquisite piece filled them, its subject led up naturally, by a swift transition, to the highest pitch of convivial jollity, in which the music no longer counts for its own sake; it was, indeed, our friend who gave the signal by springing up from the piano, advancing towards Franziska, and persuading her to join in a *Schleifer*, or slow gliding waltz, while Max picked up his violin with the greatest alacrity. Nor was their host behind hand in inviting Madame Mozart. In a twinkling all the portable furniture was removed by the bustling servants in order to make more room. One after the other each had to take a turn, and the maiden aunt, by no means loth, was led out by the gallant lieutenant in a minuet, during which she became quite rejuvenated. And lastly, as Mozart was dancing the final round with the future bride, he helped himself in style to his promised right from her fair lips.

Evening had now overtaken them, the sun was about to set, and now at last it was growing pleasant out of doors, so the Countess proposed to the ladies that they should take a breath of air in the garden. The Count, on the other hand, invited the gentlemen into the billiard-room, for Mozart was known to be very fond of that game. They accordingly separated into two parties, and for our part we will join the ladies.

Having sauntered once or twice at an easy pace up and down the main avenue, they ascended a rounded hillock, half surrounded by a tall vine-covered trellis, from which there was a view out over the open country, the village and highroad. The last rays of autumn sunshine glowed red through the leafy vines.

'Would this not be a nice place to sit down cosily,' said the Countess, 'if Madame Mozart would be so good as to tell us some story about herself and her husband?'

She was quite ready and willing, and they all settled down most comfortably, having drawn up their chairs into a circle.

'I am going to regale you,' she began, 'with a story that you would in any case have been bound to hear, for there is a little joke connected with it which I am saving up for you. It has occurred to me that, in remembrance of this occasion, I might offer a wedding-present of the most choice quality to her ladyship who is soon to be married. The said present is anything but an article of luxury or fashion, so it is perhaps only by reason of its history that it may be of some interest to you.'

'What can it be, Eugenie?' said Franziska. 'Some celebrity's inkstand, at the very least!'

'You are not so very far out! You shall see it within the very hour! The treasure is in our travelling-trunk. I will begin, and, with your permission, I will hark back a little way.'

'The winter before last, the state of Mozart's health threatened to give me serious cause for alarm, by reason of his growing irritability and frequent fits of depression – a febrile state, in fact. Though still at times lively in society, often more than was really natural, at home he was generally absorbed in gloomy broodings, sighing and complaining. The doctor ordered dieting. Pyrmont water, and exercise outside the city. But the patient did not pay much attention to this good advice; the cure was inconvenient, wasted time, and was dead against his usual daily routine. Well, the doctor made things nice and hot for him, and he had to listen to a long lecture on the composition of human blood and those corpuscle things in it, on respiration and phlogiston – I declare, you never heard the like of it all! – or again, on Nature's real intentions with regard to food, drink and digestion, a thing about which Mozart had till that time been about as innocent as his own five-year-old boy. As a matter of fact, the lecture produced a visible impression. The doctor had not been half an hour gone when I found my husband in his room gazing meditatively, though with a more cheerful face, at a walking-stick for which he had been rummaging in a press among some old things, and had successfully found it. I should never have thought that he would even have remembered its existence. It had come down to us from my father, and was a handsome cane with an imposing knob of lapis lazuli. Never had a walking-stick been seen in Mozart's hand before. I simply had to laugh.

' "You see, " he cried, "I am going in for my cure thoroughly, with all its appurtenances. I intend to drink the water, take exercise every day in the open air, and, in doing so, make use of this staff. And apropos of sticks, all sorts of ideas have been passing through my head. It is not for nothing,

then, I thought, that other people – I mean real, steady-going fellows – cannot go without a walking-stick. Our neighbour the commercial councillor never crosses the street to visit his old cronies, but his stick must go with him. Professional men and officials, gentlemen in government offices, tradesmen and their customers, when they take a walk outside the city on a Sunday with their families – every one of them carries his good honest cane that has seen good service. But chief of all, I have often observed how on the Stefansplatz in front of the Cathedral, about half an hour before the sermon begins, or Mass, the respectable citizens stand about chatting in groups: and there one can see quite plainly how all and sundry of their quiet virtues, their industry and sense of order, their serene courage and contentment, depend upon their trusty stick and prop themselves up by its steady support. In a word, there must be something beneficial, some special consolation to be found in this old-world and perhaps rather unfashionable custom. Believe me or not, I can hardly wait for the first occasion when I shall take this good friend for a walk across the bridge of the Rennweg as part of my certificate of health. We are already slightly acquainted, and I hope the alliance we have concluded will be for all time.''

'But the alliance proved of brief duration; the third time the two of them went out together, his companion failed to return. Another was procured, which kept faith a little longer, and at any rate it is to this fancy for walking-sticks that I put down a great deal of the assiduity with which Mozart followed out his doctor's prescription quite tolerably well for three whole weeks. Nor were good results lacking; hardly ever had we seen him so fresh and bright or so even-tempered. But in a short time, alas! he had grown far too frisky again, so that every day I had my hands full with him. About this time it happened that, wearied by the labours of an exacting day, he none the less went rather late to a musical party for the benefit of a few curious travellers, though he vowed by all that was holy that it should by only for an hour; but those are always the occasions when, once he is stuck down at the piano and thoroughly roused, people take the most shameful advantage of his good nature; for at such times he sits there like the little fellow in Montgolfier's air-balloon, floating six miles up above

the earth, where one cannot so much as hear the bells ring. I sent our man round twice in the middle of the night, but it was no use, he could not get at his master. About three in the morning he at last got home. So I made up my mind to sulk hard all day.'

At this point certain circumstances were passed over by Madame Mozart in silence. It should be known that a young singer, Signora Malerbi, to whom Frau Konstanze took exception with good cause, was most likely to be present as well at the above-mentioned evening party. This Roman lady owed her engagement at the opera-house to Mozart's good offices; and her coquettish wiles had undoubtedly had no small share in winning the Master's favour. There were even rumours that she had had him in her toils for several months past, and kept him nicely on the rack. But whether this was altogether true, or greatly exaggerated, it is certain that she behaved later with insolence and ingratitude, and even went so far as to make fun of her benefactor. Thus it was quite in her own characteristic vein when once, in speaking to another and more fortunate admirer, she roundly called him 'un piccolo grifo raso' (a shaven little pig's snout). This inspiration worthy of a Circe was all the more calculated to wound him because, as we are bound to admit, it contained, after all, a germ of truth.

On the way home from this party, at which it so happened, however, that the singer had failed to appear, a friend, heated by wine, was indiscreet enough to repeat her spiteful remark to the Master. He was not best pleased at this, for, as a matter of fact, it was the first unequivocal proof he had received of his protégée's utter heartlessness. So bitter was his indignation that at first he did not even notice the chilly reception with which he met at his wife's bedside. Without pausing to draw breath he told her of the insult, and his honesty would lead us to infer that his conscience was not so very guilty. She was almost moved to pity him. But she purposely did violence to her feelings, for she did not intend him to get off so easily as all that. When, shortly after midday, he woke from a heavy sleep, he found that both his wife and the two children had gone out, though the table was neatly laid for him alone.

Few things had ever made Mozart so unhappy as when everything was not perfectly smooth and serene between him and his better half. And had he only known, too, what further cause for anxiety she had been carrying about with her for many days past! – one of the most serious causes, indeed, the disclosure of which, according to her long-standing custom, she was sparing him as long as possible. Her ready money would quite shortly be at an end, and there was no prospect of anything coming in for some time yet. Though he had no suspicion of this domestic crisis, yet his heart, too, suffered from a sense of oppression having some affinity with her distressed and embarrassed condition. He could neither eat nor remain still. He hastily finished dressing, if only so as to escape from the stifling atmosphere of the house. On a scrap of paper, which he left unfolded, he wrote a few lines in Italian: 'You have made me take my medicine, and it serves me thoroughly well right. But do be nice again and be ready to laugh once more by the time I come home. I feel I could turn Carthusian and Trappist. I declare, I could bellow like a bull of Bashan!' He promptly snatched up his hat, but not the stick with it this time; its day was now over.

Having acted as substitute for Frau Konstanze thus far in her story, we may as well proceed a little further.

Leaving his home near the Schranne (the Market hall) and turning to the right opposite the Zeughaus (the Armoury), the good man, musing idly, sauntered – for it was a warm, rather cloudy summer's afternoon – across what is known as the Hof, and on past the priest's house adjoining the Church of Our Lady, in the direction of the Schottentor, where he turned off to the left and climbed up to the Mölkerbastei, thus avoiding the greetings of a number of acquaintances who were just entering the city. Though unmolested by a guard who was pacing up and down by the cannon, he paused here only a short time to enjoy the splendid view out over the green slope of the glacis and past the outskirts of the town to the Kahlenberg and southwards towards the Styrian Alps. The fair peace of Nature was out of harmony with his inward state. With a sigh he proceeded on his way across the esplanade and then through the suburb known as the Alser-Vorstadt, walking quite at random.

At the end of the Währinger Gasse stood a tavern with a skittle-alley, the proprietor of which, a rope-maker, was very well known in the neighbourhood, as well as to the country-folk whose road led them past the house, both for the quality of his wares and the soundness of his liquor. The roll of skittles was to be heard, and besides, since the house could muster a dozen clients at most, the business done there was fairly quiet. An almost unconscious craving to lose himself in something external to him, among unassuming, natural people, prompted the Master to walk in. He sat down at one of the tables, sparsely shaded by trees, with a chief inspector of wells from Vienna and two other stodgy citizens, ordered a small mug of beer, and entered into every detail of their very workaday conversation, from time to time taking a stroll round or watching the game in the skittle-alley.

Not far from the latter, by the side of the house, the rope-maker's shop stood open, a narrow space stuffed full of his wares, where, in addition to the immediate products of his craft, every variety of implement for kitchen, cellar or farm stood or hung about the shop for sale, likewise train-oil and axle-grease, as well as a few varieties of seeds, dill and caraway. A young girl, who had to act as waitress to the customers as well as attend to the shop, happened at the moment to be busy serving a peasant, who had looked in, with his little son clinging to his hand, to buy a bushel-measure for fruit, a brush, a whip or something of the kind. He picked one out from among a number of them, tried it, laid it aside, took up a second and a third, then returned irresolutely to the first, and could not make an end of it all. Several times the girl went out to wait on her clients, then she came back again, and was untiring in assisting his choice and giving him satisfaction without overmuch talk.

Seated on a low bench by the skittle-alley, Mozart was watching the whole thing and listening delightedly. Though greatly pleased with the girl's good-natured, sensible bearing and the calm, serious expression of her attractive face, he was still more interested in the peasant, who afforded him much food for thought even after he had gone off in a high state of contentment. He had entered thoroughly into the man's point of view, sensing what importance he had attached to this trifling occasion, and with what conscientious care he had chaffered over the price, though the difference involved was only a few farthings. 'And then,' he mused, 'only think when the fellow gets home to his wife, and boasts to her of his bargain, and the children all hang round till his knapsack is opened, in case there is something in it for them; but she hurries to fetch him a snack and a cool draught of this season's home-brewed cider, for which he has been saving up his appetite.

'Who would not be as happy as this man – so independent of mankind, looking only to Nature and her blessings, hardly though she makes him earn them!

'But in my art the task that is set me daily is quite different, and, when all is said and done, I would not exchange it with anyone in the world. Yet in the meantime why do I have to live under conditions in such direct contrast with this innocent, simple existence? Supposing, now, you had a bit of land, a little house near a village in a beautiful neighbourhood, you really could not help gaining a new lease of life! The whole morning busy over your scores, and all the rest of the time with your family, planting trees, going round your field, and in the autumn shaking down the apples and pears with the children; a visit to town now and then for some performance, and, for the rest, a friend or so to stay from time to time – what bliss! Well, well, who knows what yet may befall?'

He walked to the front of the shop, said a few kindly words to the girl, and began to look more closely at her wares. Apart from the direct bearing of these objects upon the idyllic trend of his thoughts, as described above, he was attracted by the neat, bright, smooth quality of all these wooden utensils, and even by the smell of them. His eye was caught by the gardening tools. For at his suggestion Konstanze had leased some time ago a little piece of land outside the Kärntner Tor and grown some green-stuff there; so the first thing that now struck him as most appropriate was a large new rake and a smaller ditto, together with a spade. For the rest, it did the greatest credit to his ideas of economy that, after a short period of reflexion, he relinquished, though regretfully, a butter-keg of the most inviting and appetizing aspect. On the other hand, a tall receptacle with a cover and a beautifully carved handle seemd to him the very thing for some purpose of which he did not feel quite sure. Composed of slender rods of two sorts of wood, light and dark alternately, it was broader at the bottom than at the top, and exquisitely finished with pitch inside. A fine assortment of ladles, rolling-pins, chopping-boards, and plates of all sizes seemed eminently desirable for the kitchen, as did also a salt-box of the simplest construction for hanging on the wall.

Lastly, his eye fell upon a sturdy walking-stick, the handle of which was well garnished with leather and round brass nails. And since her customer seemed rather tempted by this too, the saleswoman remarked with a smile that it was not at all the sort of thing for a gentleman to carry. 'You are right, my child,' he replied, 'I seem to remember that butchers on their travels carry something of the kind. Away with it! I will have none of it. But on the other hand, all the rest of what we have chosen there you shall bring to my house to-day or to-morrow.' He then told her his name and street, after which he went back to his table to finish his drink, where he found only one of the three still sitting, a master tinsmith.

'The waitress has done well to-day,' remarked the man. 'Her cousin allows her a penny in the florin on what she sells in the shop.'

Mozart was now doubly pleased with his purchase; but his personal interest was to be still further heightened. For next time she came their way this same citizen called out to her: 'How goes it, Kreszenz? What is the locksmith doing? Isn't he soon to be filing his own iron?'

'Oh, rubbish!' she retorted as she hurried away again, 'any iron of his, I reckon, is still growing right back there in the mountains.'

'She's a decent girl,' said the tinsmith. 'She kept house for her stepfather for a long time and nursed him when he was ill, and then, when he died, it turned out that he had squandered her portion. Since then she has been working for her kinsman here, and she is the mainstay of the whole concern, tavern, children and all. She knows a worthy fellow, and would be glad to marry him, the sooner the better. But there is a hitch in the affair.'

'What sort of a hitch? I suppose he has no means?'

'Both of them have some savings, but not quite enough. Now there is a half-share in a house and workshop that will shortly be put up at auction in the town. The rope-maker could easily advance them what they still require to make up the deposit-money, but he naturally does not want to let the girl go, and he has good friends on the Council and the Guild, so that the young fellow meets with nothing but difficulties on every side.'

'Damnation!' burst out Mozart, so that the other man started and looked round to see whether anybody was listening. 'So there is not a soul to put in a word in the cause of justice, or shake his fist in these gentlemen's faces? The rogues! But only wait! We will trip you up yet!'

The tinsmith sat as though on thorns. He clumsily tried to tone down what he had said, and almost took the whole thing back. But Mozart refused to listen. 'Shame on you,' he said, 'for the way you talk. That's the way you miserable fellows always go on, as soon as you are called upon to stand by what you have said.' And without bidding him good day, he turned his back on the craven. As he passed by the waitress, who had her hands full with some new customers, all he did was to whisper: 'Come tomorrow in good time. My greetings to your young man. I hope your affairs will turn out well.' She only started, and had neither the time nor the presence of mind to thank him.

Walking at a faster pace than usual, for this incident had fairly made his blood boil, he first followed the same way as that by which he had come, as far as the glacis, after which he slackened his pace, taking a roundabout course which led in a wide semicircle round by the ramparts. Entirely absorbed in the affairs of the unhappy lovers, he ran over in his mind a number of his acquaintances and patrons who might be able to do something in the matter in one way or another. But in the meanwhile, since some more precise explanation from the girl was desirable before he made up his mind to take any steps, he resolved to wait quietly till it came, and now, his heart and mind outrunning his feet, he felt himself already at home with his wife.

He felt an inward certainty that he might count upon an amiable, and even a glad welcome, with a kiss and embrace upon the very threshold, and as he entered the Kärntner Tor longing redoubled his speed. Not far from there he was hailed by the postman, who handed him a small, but heavy packet, on which he instantly recognized a precise and honoured handwriting. He stepped aside with the postman into the nearest shop to sign the receipt, but once back in the street he could not wait till he reached home; he broke the seal, and, now walking, now stopping still, devoured the letter.

'I was sitting at my work-table,' said Madame Mozart, continuing her story to the ladies, 'and heard my husband come upstairs and ask our man where I was. His step and his voice sounded more cheerful and assured than I had expected, or than I was really pleased to hear. First he went to his own room, but he came across to me at once. "Good evening," he said; and without looking up I answered in a doleful voice. Having paced up and down the room in silence once or twice, with an attempt at a yawn he took up the fly-whisk from behind the door, a thing which it had never entered his head to do before, and muttering to himself: "Where on earth do all the flies come from, I wonder!" he began slapping to right and left, as hard as he could go, too. For that tone of voice was always one which he simply could not bear, so that I never ventured to use it in his presence. "Hm!" I thought, "So what one may do oneself is quite another thing when the men do it!" Besides, I had really not noticed so many flies as all that. His odd behaviour really vexed me very much. "Six at one go!" he cried. "Only look!" – No answer. Next he laid something on my pin-cushion, so that I could not help seeing it even without moving my eyes from my work. It was nothing more alarming that a little pile of gold, as many ducats as one can pick up between thumb and finger. He went on with his antics behind my back, making an occasional slap and talking to himself all the while: "The tiresome, useless, impudent brood! For whatever purpose do they exist on earth, I wonder?" – Slap! "Just so that one may kill them, evidently!" – Slap! – "and I must say I am a pretty good hand at it, too. Natural history tells us at what an astounding rate the creatures multiply!" – Slap! slap! – "but in my house they will always be cleared out at once! *Ah maledette! Disperate!* Despair, you wretches! Another twenty again, all together! Do you like them?" He came up to me again, and did the same thing as before. Up to this point I had restrained my laughter by an effort, but I could simply do so no longer; I exploded, he fell on my neck, and we both tittered and laughed away as though for a wager.

' "But where did the money come from?" I asked, while he shook the rest of it out of the little roll. "From Prince Eszterhazy! Through Haydn! Only read the letter!" And this is what I read:

' "Eisenstadt, etc., etc. Dearest Friend, His Serene Highness, my most gracious lord, has to my very great delight commissioned me to convey to you the accompanying sixty ducats. We have recently performed your quartets again, and His Serene Highness was, if anything, even more struck with them and pleased than he was the first time, three months ago. The prince remarked to me (I must write down his very words): 'When Mozart dedicated this work to you, he meant to honour you alone; but he cannot take it amiss if at the same time I see in it a compliment to myself. Tell him that I have almost as high an opinion of his genius as you have yourself, and more than that he could hardly ask.' 'Amen to that!' is what I say. Are you content?

' "Postscript: a word in your charming wife's ear: kindly see to it that there is no delay in returning thanks. It would be best if this could be done in person. We should take care not to lose such a favourable wind." '

' "Angelic messenger! Celestial soul!" exclaimed Mozart over and over again, and it is hard to say which pleased him most, the letter, the Prince's approbation, or the money. For my own part, I frankly confess that at that precise moment the last-mentioned appeared to me extremely timely. And so we passed a most festive and happy evening.

'As to the adventure in the Alser-Vorstadt, I heard nothing that day and equally little during the next few either. The whole of the next week slipped past, no Kreszenz appeared, and in the turmoil of his affairs my husband forgot all about the matter. One Sunday evening we were entertaining company: Captain Wesselt, Count Hardegg and others were taking part in some music. During a pause I was called out of the room – and there was the whole bag of tricks! I went in and enquired "Did you order all sorts of wooden goods from the Alser-Vorstadt?" "Great Heavens, yes, so I did! Isn't there a girl there? Just ask her in." So in she came as pleasant as could be, bringing her loaded basket into the room on her arm, and the rakes and spade and all. She apologized for having been such a long time coming, but she had been unable to recall the name of the street, and had failed to ascertain it exactly till that very day. Mozart took the things from her one after the other, handing them over to me as he did so, and looking so pleased with himself. I feigned delight and thanked him most heartily, praising and commending everything, but I could not help wondering why he had bought the gardening-tools. – "Why, naturally," said he, "for your little bit of land on the banks of the Wien." "Good Heavens! But we gave that up long ago! The water always did so much damage, and besides, we never got anything whatever to grow there. I told you all about it, and you made no objection." "What! And so the asparagus we ate this spring?" "All came from the market!" "There!" he said, "If only I had known! I only praised it so out of pure politeness, for I was really touched at you and your gardening. Such miserable little heads they were, no bigger than so many quills!"

'The gentlemen enjoyed the joke beyond words. I had promptly to hand over the superfluous objects to some of them as keepsakes. But when Mozart went on to question the girl about how matters stood with regard to her marriage, she plucked up courage to speak out quite freely, for anything that was to be done for her and her young man must be done quietly, discreetly and without giving anybody grounds for complaint – all of which she expressed with such modesty, prudence and forbearance that she quite won the approval of all present, and was finally sent off with the most encouraging promises.

' "These people have got to be helped," said the Captain. "The business with the Guild is the least part of the trouble, for I know somebody who will soon set that to rights. The question is how to pay something on account for the house, the expenses of setting up business and so forth. How would it be if we were to announce a concert, among friends, at Trattnern's hall, everybody paying as much as he likes for his ticket?" The idea was greeted with vigorous applause. One of the gentlemen picked up the salt-box, saying: "Somebody ought to open proceedings with a nice historical discourse, describing Herr Mozart's purchases and explaining his humane intentions, at which point this handsome receptacle should be set on the table as a collecting box, with the two rakes to right and left, and crossed behind it as a decoration."

'This did not happen, of course; but on the other hand the concert did take place. It brought in a nice sum and various contributions came in afterwards, so that the happy couple had enough and to spare, and the other obstacles were soon overcome. The Duscheks in Prague, our greatest friends there, with whom we usually stay, heard the story, and she, being a most good-natured, kind-hearted woman, asked to have one of the things too, out of curiosity; so I set aside the most suitable pieces for her, and took this opportunity of bringing them with me. But since in the meantime we have unexpectedly chanced to discover a new and delightful fellow-artist, who is very shortly to set up a house of her own, and will not, I think, despise a piece of common household gear chosen by Mozart, I mean to halve what I have brought, and you have the choice between a handsome open-work chocolate-whisk and the much-talked-of salt-box, upon which the artist has indulged himself with the luxury of a tasteful tulip. I should certainly advise you to choose this piece, for salt, that noble commodity, is, I believe, a symbol of home and hospitality, to which we should like to add all our good wishes.'

Thus ended Madame Mozart's story. We may imagine with what merriment the ladies heard it, and how gratefully the present was accepted. The jubilation was renewed when immediately afterwards the things were set out before them and the men upstairs, and the emblem of patriarchal simplicity was formally presented, whereupon the young lady's uncle promised it a place in its new owner's plate-chest and in that of her remotest posterity in no whit inferior to that occupied in the collection at Ambras by the Florentine master's famous work of art.

By this time it was nearly eight o'clock, and they had tea. But soon our musician was urgently reminded of the promise he had already given at midday to make the company better acquainted with the 'rake-hell' hero (*Höllenbrand*) who lay under lock and key in the travelling-trunk, though fortunately not too deep down. Without the least reluctance he declared himself in readiness. His explanation of the plot did not detain them long, the book of words was opened, and the candles stood, ready lighted, on the pianoforte.

We only wish that something, at least, might be communicated to our readers of that rare emotion which often thrills us, as though by an electric shock, and holds us, as it were, spellbound, when, as we pass by a window,

a single isolated chord is borne to our ears – a chord that could come from there alone; something of that sweet, yet painful suspense with which we sit facing the curtain at the theatre while the orchestra is tuning up. Or is it not something in this fashion? If on the threshold of every work of sublimely tragic art, be it Macbeth, Œdipus or any other, we feel the pulsing tremor of eternal beauty, where else should this have been intenser than now, or even of equal potency? Man at once longs and dreads to be rapt out of his ordinary self; he feels the approaching contact with the infinite and how it constricts his breast, though its purpose, all the while, is to expand it and ravish his spirit by its might. Add to this his awe in the presence of consummate art; the thought that it is granted him to enjoy a god-like marvel, to assimilate it as a thing akin to himself, induces a sort of emotion, or even pride, the happiest and purest, perhaps, of which we are capable.

But added to all this, our company was now, for the first time, to become acquainted with a work which we have made entirely our own from youth upwards, a state poles apart from ours, and, if we allow for the enviable pleasure of a personal rendering by the composer himself, one by no means as favourable as that which we enjoy, for a distinct and perfect conception of the piece was really impossible for any of them, nor could they have had this, for more reasons than one, even if the whole piece could have been presented to them without abbreviation.

Of the eighteen numbers already fully completed the composer presumably did not perform even half (in the account upon which our narrative is based we find expressly mentioned only the last piece in this series, the sextet); he rendered them it seems, for the most part, in a free version for piano only, chiming in with his voice when necessary and suitable. As for his wife, she is recorded only as performing two airs. Since her voice is said to have been as strong as it was lovely, we should like to think that these were Donna Anna's first song, *Or sai, chi l'onore* and one of the two sung by Zerlina. Strictly speaking, so far as intelligence and taste were concerned, Eugenie and her betrothed were the only listeners of the type which the Master would naturally have desired, and the former was, without a doubt, incomparably more so than the latter. They both sat at the far end of the room, the young lady immobile as a statue, and so profoundly absorbed in the music, that, even during the brief intervals in which the interest of the others found shy expression, or their inward emotion involuntarily escaped them in a cry of admiration, she could give none but an inadequate reply to the remarks addressed to her by her betrothed.

When Mozart reached the end of the incomparably lovely sextet, which was the occasion for a prolonged discussion, he seemed to listen with special interest and gratification to certain observations of the Baron's. They were speaking of the finale of the opera, and also of the performance, which had been provisionally fixed for the beginning of November; and somebody having expressed the opinion that certain parts of the finale might yet cost the Master enormous trouble, he gave rather a cryptic smile. But Konstanze said out loud to the Countess, in such a way that he could not have helped hearing: 'He has something still *in petto* that he is keeping a secret even from me.'

'You are departing from your usual rôle, my love,' he rejoined, 'in bringing up that point; only supposing I took it into my head to start all over again! And as a matter of fact, I am itching to do so.'

'Leporello!' cried the Count, springing jovially to his feet, and signing to a servant, 'Wine! Sillery, three bottles!'

'Oh no, please! The time for that is past. My lord and master has not recovered from the last yet.'

'May it do him good! And the same for all of us!'

'Heavens! what have I done?' lamented Konstanze with a glance at the clock. 'It is already eleven, and we have to start early in the morning. How is it to be done?'

'It can't be done, dear friend, it seems to me. No it positively can't.'

'Yet at times,' began Mozart, 'things fall out remarkably aptly. But what will my Stanzerl say, now, when she hears that the piece of work she is about to hear was born into the world at about this very time of night, and just before a journey was arranged, too?'

'Is it possible? When? Three weeks ago, I warrant, when you were going to Eisenstadt?'

'Right! And this is how it happened. After ten o'clock, when you were already sound asleep, I came home from Richter's dinner, and meant to go to bed in good time, as I had promised, so as to be up early in the morning and take my place in the carriage. Meanwhile Veit, as usual, had lighted the candles on my writing-table, so I slipped on my dressing-gown mechanically, and it occurred to me to take just a hasty peep at my last piece of work again. But alas! by ill-luck – O accursed and most untimely fussi-

ness of women! – you had tidied up and packed my music – for of course
I had to take it with me; the Prince wished me to try the opus through. I
hunted about, grumbled, scolded, but in vain! In the midst of all this, my
eye was caught by a sealed envelope, from the Abbate, to judge from the
appalling scrawl in which it was addressed. Yes, sure enough it was, send-
ing me the rest of his libretto, duly revised, which I had not hoped to see
for a whole month to come. I sat down at once all agog and read it through,
and was enchanted to see how well the queer fish had grasped what I
wanted. It was all far simpler and more concentrated, and at the same time
there was more in it. Both the churchyard scene and the finale, down to
where the hero descends into the underworld, were greatly improved in
every way. ''But this time, my admirable, poet'' I thought, ''you shall not
conjure up heaven and hell for me again and get no thanks for it!'' Now
as a rule it is not my custom to compose anything out of its order, however
tempting it may be; it is always a bad habit, which may be punished most
unpleasantly. But there are exceptions, and, to be brief, the scene before
the equestrian statue of the Commendatore and the threat which, issuing
from the murdered man's grave, breaks abruptly into the laughter of the
nocturnal reveller with hair-raising effect, had already gone to my head.
I struck a chord, and felt that I was knocking at the right door, behind
which, one beside the other, lay the whole legion of terrors let loose in the
finale. Well the first to come forth was an adagio: D minor, four bars only,
followed by a second phrase in five – I flatter myself it will produce an
extraordinary effect in the theatre, when the most powerful of the wind-
instruments accompany the voice.[1] Only listen now, as well as I can manage
it here.'

Without more ado he put out the lights in the two branched candlesticks
standing by his side, and the grim chorale *Di rider finirai pria dell'aurora*
rang through the death-like stillness of the room. As though borne from
the orbits of far-distant stars, the notes come dropping from trombones

---

[1] Translator's note – In connexion with this passage it may be recalled that, as
related by Jahn, *Life of Mozart* (trs. Townshend), III, 130, 'The words of the
Commendatore in the churchyard scene were originally, it is said, accompanied
only by the trombones.'

of silver, ice-cold and piercing through both heart and marrow, down
through the blue night.

'*Chi va la?* Who goes there? Reply!' we hear Don Juan ask. Then the
voice rings out again in the same monotone, ordering the impious youth to
leave the dead in peace.

When these booming accents had died away on the air down to the very
last vibration, Mozart went on: 'You can understand that there was no
stopping now. Once the ice cracks at one point of the shore, the whole
surface of the lake breaks up at once and the crash echoes even unto its
remotest corner. Involuntarily I gathered up the same threads later on, at
Don Giovanni's supper-party, where Donna Elvira has just gone out, and
the ghost appears in response to his invitation. Listen to this!'

Now followed the whole of that long and fearful dialogue by which even
the most matter-of-fact of men is swept away to the farthest confines of
what the human mind can conceive, yea, and beyond, to where we look
upon the supernatural and hear its voice, and feel ourselves, within our in-
most breast, bereft of will and hurled from one extreme to another.

Though already alien to human utterance, the deathless voice of the de-
parted deigns once more to speak. Shortly after the first dread salutation,
when, already half immortal, he scorns the proffered earthly food, with
what uncanny, gruesome effect does his voice stray up and down the
strange intervals of an aerial scale, as on some ladder woven of air! He
calls for a speedy decision to repent; for the time accorded him is short,
and far, far, far is the way! And when Don Giovanni, defying the eternal
ordinances in his monstrous contumacy, struggles distractedly, grapples and
writhes under the growing onslaughts of the infernal powers, and finally
sinks downwards, still expressing in his every gesture the fulness of his
majesty, what man is there whose heart, and whose very entrails are not
stirred by mingled terror and delight? The emotion may be compared to
that with which we gaze in wonder on the glorious spectacle of some un-
governable force of Nature, or a fire on board some splendid ship. In spite
of ourselves we take sides, as it were, with its blind might, and gnash our
teeth as we share its travail in the anguished process of its self-destruction.

The composer had reached the end. For a while none dared be first to break the general silence.

'Give us,' began the Countess at last, still with a catch in her breath, 'Give us, pray, some idea of what your feelings were as you laid down your pen that night.'

He looked at her with shining eyes, as though roused from some tranquil reverie, rapidly collected his thoughts, and said, half to the lady and half to his wife: 'Well, by the end of it all, my head was simply reeling. I had written away at this desperate *dibattimento* down to the chorus of spirits, going straight on in a perfect fever as I sat beside the open window, till it was finished, and after a short pause I rose from my chair, intending to go to your room so that we might chat a while longer till my blood had subsided. But now an idea flashed through my mind and brought me up short in the middle of the room.' At this point he glanced down at the ground for a couple of seconds, and during what followed his voice betrayed an almost imperceptible agitation. 'I said to myself: "supposing, now, you were to die to-night, and had to break off your score at this point: would it let you rest quiet in your grave?" My eye fell on the wick of the candle I was carrying, and the mountains of wax that had dripped from it. A momentary pang ran through me at this idea; then I bethought myself again: "but supposing that some time afterwards, be it long or short, some other man, perhaps some Italian fellow, were to get hold of the opera to complete it, and found the whole thing neatly put together, from the introduction to the seventeenth number, with the exception of a single piece – fine, sound, ripe fruits shaken down into the long grass, so that all he need do was to pick them up – yet all the same, he was feeling a little bit nervous about the middle of the finale here – and then, at that very moment, he discovered that this solid mass of rock had already been moved thus far out of his way: that would give him something over which he well might chuckle! He might perhaps be tempted to cheat me of the honour and glory. But he would be sure to burn his fingers nicely if he did; for, after all, there would still be some few of my good friends able to recognize my sign manual, who would see to it that I received my due." So I went and thanked

God, with my eyes turned heavenward in heartfelt gratitude; and gave thanks, too, dear wife, to your good angel, who had kept both his hands laid softly on your brow for so long that you went on sleeping like a dormouse and could not call out to me so much as once. But when I did come to you at last and was asked what time it was, without turning a hair I mendaciously made you out an hour or two younger than you really were, for it was close on four o'clock. And now you will understand why it was that you could not get me out of bed at six, so that the coachman had to be sent home and ordered again for the next day.'

'Of course,' retorted Konstanze, 'but the sly fellow need not imagine that a body was so dense as not to notice anything! So there was really no need for you to keep your splendid spurt forward a secret!'

'Ah, but that was not the reason.'

'I know – you wanted to keep your treasure to yourself for a while, and not have everybody exclaiming over it.'

'I am only glad,' cried their good-natured host, 'that to-morrow we need not wound the noble heart of any Viennese coachman, supposing that Herr Mozart proves quite incapable of getting up. The order: "Hans, unharness the horses again!" always upsets people.'

This indirect invitation to prolong their stay, in which all the others joined their voices in the most cordial and pressing manner, led the travellers to explain their very cogent reasons to the contrary; but one point was readily agreed upon: that they must not start too early, but must stay long enough to enjoy a comfortable breakfast together.

For some time longer they continued to stand or drift about in groups talking. Mozart was looking for somebody, apparently for the future bride; but since she did not happen to be there at the moment, he naïvely put the question intended for her directly to Franziska, who was standing close by: 'Well, and what did you think of our Don Giovanni on the whole? What good fortune can you prophesy for him?'

'I will try,' she rejoined with a laugh, 'to answer as well as I can in place of my cousin. My untutored opinion is this: that if Don Giovanni does not turn the heads of the whole world, then the good God may shut up his musical-box, for an indefinite period, that is, and give humanity to understand. . . .' 'And give humanity,' corrected her uncle, 'a bagpipes to carry; and harden men's hearts so that they worship strange gods.'

'Heaven preserve us!' laughed Mozart. 'But there! in the course of the next sixty or seventy years, when I am long dead and gone, many a false prophet shall arise.'

Eugenie came up with the Baron and Max, and imperceptibly the conversation took a fresh turn, once more becoming grave and weighty, so that before the company dispersed again, the composer had the pleasure of hearing a number of fine and pregnant observations of a kind flattering to his hopes.

It was long after midnight before they dispersed; for till then none of them had realized how greatly they needed rest.

On the following day, the weather being in no way inferior to that of the day before, by ten o'clock a smart travelling-carriage, packed with the belongings of the two guests from Vienna, was seen standing in the courtyard of the Schloss. The Count stood before it with Mozart, shortly before the horses were led out, and asked him how he liked it.

'Very much. It seems extremely comfortable.'

'Good! Then will you give me the pleasure of keeping it as a remembrance of me?'

'What! Are you in earnest?'

'How could I be otherwise?'

'Holy Saints! Konstanze! Here!' he called up to the window from which she was looking out with the others. 'The carriage is for me! In future you shall ride in your own carriage!'

He threw his arms round the donor, who was smiling broadly, then walked round his new property, looking at it from every point of view, opened the door, threw himself down inside, and called out to them: 'I feel as grand and distinguished as the Chevalier Gluck! Won't they stare in Vienna!'

'I hope,' said the Countess, 'that on your way back from Prague we shall see your conveyance all begarlanded with wreaths.'

Not long after this merry scene, the carriage which had been the subject of so many eulogies really began to move off, and, drawn by a smart pair, drove at a brisk trot down to the main road. The Count sent his own horses with them as far as Wittingau, where they were to hire post-horses.

When good, kind people have enlivened our house with their presence for a while, bringing a fresh and quickened stir of life into our existence by their invigorating mental atmosphere, and causing us to experience to the full the blessedness of hospitality, their departure always leaves us with a comfortless sense of flatness for the rest of the day, at least – supposing, that is, that we are entirely thrown back upon our own resources again.

But this last condition, at least, did not affect the party at the Schloss. Franziska's parents, it is true, and the old aunt with them, also took their departure immediately afterwards; but the young lady herself and the future bridegroom remained behind, to say nothing of Max. As for Eugenie, with whom we are here more particularly concerned, this superlatively precious experience had affected her more deeply than all the rest, so it might well be imagined that she could find nothing wanting, nothing amiss, and nothing that could damp her joy. Her perfect happiness in the man she truly loved had just received its formal sanction, and this could not fail to outweigh everything else; indeed this, the noblest and most beautiful experience that could have moved her heart, was fused inevitably with the fulness of her bliss. Or it would have been had she been able to live that day and the one before only in the present, and afterwards in nothing but the pure enjoyment of its after-effects. But already during the evening, while his wife had been telling her story, a slight dread had come over her on behalf of him whose lovable presentment was then delighting her. This premonition still agitated the lower depths of her consciousness all the while Mozart was playing, looming through all the ineffable charm and mysterious horror of the music; and finally the anecdote with the same suggestion that he had casually related about himself had surprised and shocked her profoundly. So sure, so absolutely certain did she feel that this man would rapidly and inevitably be consumed away in the flame of his own ardour, that he could not possibly be more than a fleeting apparition upon earth, if only because this world was in truth incapable of bearing the overwhelming richness of that which he would lavish upon it.

This and much more beside had ebbed and flowed in her bosom on the previous day, while the confused echoes of Don Giovanni were still reverberating in her inward ear. It was not till towards morning that she fell asleep, worn out with fatigue.

The three ladies had now settled down with their work in the garden, and the men were keeping them company; since the conversation naturally turned at first upon no other subject than Mozart, Eugenie made no secret of her fears. Nobody was in the least inclined to share them, though the Baron entered into them to the full. In hours of happiness and moods of sheer human emotion and gratitude, men are wont to brush aside with all their might any thoughts of disaster that do not directly affect themselves· The most forcible and tempting proofs to the contrary were put forward, especially by her uncle, and how gladly did Eugenie listen to them all! A little more and she would really have been convinced that she had seen things in too gloomy a light.

A few moments later, as she passed through the great saloon upstairs, which had just been cleaned and set to rights again, and whose green damask curtains, now drawn across the window, admitted only a soft twilight gloom, she paused sadly before the piano. She gazed long and thoughtfully down at the keys which he had been the last to touch, then softly closed the lid and turned the key with jealous care, so that no other hand should open it again for a long time to come. As she turned away, she chanced to put a few song-books back in their right place. An old sheet of paper fell out, a copy of a Bohemian folk-song that Franziska had often sung in earlier days, and she herself too. She picked it up, though not before she had stepped upon it. In such a mood as hers, the most natural occurrence may easily appear a portent. But however she might interpret it, the tenour of the song was such that, as she once more perused the simple verses, hot tears fell from her eyes.

A little fir-tree green,
Somewhere in the forest;
A rose-tree – who shall say
In what rose-garden?
– Already are they chosen,
My soul, ah, ponder!
To root upon thy grave,
And there to flourish.

A pair of black colts, grazing
In yonder meadow,
Speed homewards to the town
And canter gaily.
– Slow shall their pacing be
Before thy coffin,
Perhaps – who knows? – ere ever
The iron shall loosen
That bright upon their hoofs
I now see gleaming.